Alone in the forest . . .

When she had made the bow and arrows, when she had bartered for the jerkin, she had told herself that it was a game. She liked to pretend to be a boy sometimes.

But it wasn't a game any longer. To go where a girl could not venture, she would travel as a boy.

It would be a long journey. The famous outlaw who was her father roamed Sherwood Forest most of the time, but wandered seldom to Barnesdale, or to the smaller forests north of Barnesdale, such as Celandine's Wood.

With her bow and arrows slung over her back and her knife and leggings tied around her waist, Rosemary shimmied down the oak, leaving what was left of her old life in the hollow.

"Good-bye," she whispered.

"Rowan Hood reads like the first in a series, and teens are sure to hope that it will be just that, leading to many more."
—*VOYA*

"The phrasing is often poetically lovely . . . the characters are memorable." —*Children's Literature*

Rowan Hood

Outlaw Girl of Sherwood Forest

Nancy Springer

PUFFIN BOOKS

PUFFIN BOOKS
Published by the Penguin Group
Penguin Putnam Books for Young Readers,
345 Hudson Street, New York, New York 10014, U.S.A.
Penguin Books Ltd, 80 Strand, London WC2R ORL, England
Penguin Books Australia Ltd, Ringwood, Victoria, Australia
Penguin Books Canada Ltd, 10 Alcorn Avenue, Toronto, Ontario, Canada M4V 3B2
Penguin Books (N.Z.) Ltd, 182-190 Wairau Road, Auckland 10, New Zealand

Penguin Books Ltd, Registered Offices: Harmondsworth, Middlesex, England

First published in the United States of America by Philomel Books,
a division of Penguin Putnam Books for Young Readers, 2001
Published by Puffin Books,
a division of Penguin Putnam Books for Young Readers, 2002

1 3 5 7 9 10 8 6 4 2

Text copyright © Nancy Springer, 2001
All rights reserved

THE LIBRARY OF CONGRESS HAS CATALOGED THE PHILOMEL EDITION AS FOLLOWS:
Rowan Hood, outlaw girl of sherwood forest / Nancy Springer.
p. cm.
Summary: In her quest to connect with Robin Hood, the father she has never
met, thirteen-year-old Rosemary disguises herself as a boy, befriends a
half-wolf, half-dog, a runaway princess, and an overgrown boy whose
singing is hypnotic, and makes peace with her elfin heritage.
ISBN: 0-399-23368-7
1. Robin Hood (Legendary character)—Juvenile fiction. [1. Robin Hood
(Legendary character)—Fiction. 2. Fathers and daughters—Fiction.
3. Sex role—Fiction. 4. Elves—Fiction. 5. Middle Ages—Fiction.
6. Adventure and adventurers—Fiction.]
I. Title.
PZ7.S76846 Ro 2001
[Fic]—dc21 00-063694

Puffin Books ISBN 0-698-11972-X

For my mother.

One

Gathering coltsfoot at the edge of the forest, pulling the plants, roots and all, with her tough steel knife, Rosemary had just straightened when she felt her mother's protection wrap around her, so strong it made her drop her basket. Mantled in her mother's power, she could do nothing but shrink to the stony ground, crouching in the furze like a rabbit, trembling, her heart beating like partridge wings. She knew she should not have been afraid, for nothing bad could happen to her in the embrace of her mother's spell. But she felt terrified, for she knew that her mother would not have sent such a spell unless something was terribly wrong.

Wolves? Was it wolves?

Willing herself to move her head, Ro looked around. Sheep grazed on a common, and beyond the common a ploughman plodded behind a team of oxen, and beyond the ploughed strips of land huddled the huts of the village where women labored all day grinding barley, and beyond the village rose the walls of the lord's stronghold. Ro looked the other way, to the forest rising like a wall, its mazy wilderness as much of a stronghold as the lord's castle. She saw only a haze of new green leaves, but she knew that almost anything might hide within it. Shadowy folk lived there, spirits in the streams, the bracken, the trees. The *aelfe,* the old ones of the hollow hills, lived there, or so it was said. Outlaws lived there. Wild boars lived there. And wolves, maybe starving and marauding after a hard winter.

And she lived there also.

Her mother's spell ended as suddenly as it had begun, cut off as if by a sword.

It should not have ended so suddenly. Or so soon.

Rosemary stood, as alert as a deer for any hint of danger. But she saw or heard nothing wrong. Plovers flew in a rain-washed springtime sky, the ploughman whistled to his team, sheep grazed, the forest stood misted in green.

Quickly, quietly, Ro slipped between the slim trunks of young rowans into the forest. Under the shelter of tall beeches and oaks she padded homeward, the skirt of her brown frock clinging to her ankles. Her bare feet made no sound on the mossy ground.

It was not wolves. It was something with sharper fangs, orange fangs of flame. Ro whiffed its gray scent on the air long before she should have smelled the smoke of her mother's hearth fire.

She broke into a run.

But there was not much left to run toward. Not much but ashes left when she got to the forest glade where she had lived all her life. Thudding across the tender meadow grass, Ro saw blackened ground, some lumps of earth where the wattle walls had stood, some charred wood still flaming. And the bitter smoke rising where the cottage should have been. That was all.

A few paces from the scorched ground, she faltered to a stop, numb, her heart trying to deny everything. Her mother had escaped, her heart tried to tell her. It was an accident, the thatch had caught fire and her mother had not been able to put it out; her mother was wandering the forest looking for her. In a moment her mother would come running and hug her. *Please, let her be alive,* Ro's heart begged, *and I will never vex her again, I will hang my mantle where it belongs, I will fetch kindling, I will sweep—*

But her mind was strong and knew better. Why would her mother have sent a spell of protection upon her if the thatch had caught fire? Instead, her mother would have sent a call for help. Whatever had happened, Ro knew, was no accident.

Already knowing what she would find, Rosemary inched closer, forcing her staring eyes to study the blackened ground. There. Hoofprints.

Horsemen.

In other words, the lord's henchmen.

Her mind tried to say that the marauders might have taken her away, but in her heart Rosemary knew: Her mother was dead. Dead when the spell of protection had ended.

Her knees weakened and would no longer support her. She folded to the ground, her thoughts like flames that leapt and twisted and would not stand still. Her mother, Celandine, a flower of a woman always dressed in green—cut down. Her mother, killed. Just for hatred. Because she was the wood-wife.

It was not the village folk who had done this. They understood the power of woods magic, they came to Celandine for salves and healing herbs and wisdom, bringing butter or a few eggs even though no payment was necessary—they knew. But the castle folk on horseback—they would never understand.

Ro wanted to weep but could not. It was as if the fire had scorched her heart and turned it as hot and hard as the stones of the cracked, ruined hearth.

Her mother. Dead.

The flames wavered and went out. Ro sat and stared at the ashes as the tree shadows shifted and embers flickered like her thoughts. Where would she go now? How would she live? It was hard to think with grief settling in her hard and heavy like a rock, but she knew she had to think if she were to survive. How to go on, how to live? There was no easy answer—not for her, a girl of thirteen.

"Well," she mumbled to herself, "I could be a privy cleaner, I suppose. Or a chimney sweep."

There were no good perchances. She could stay where she was, in the forest glade with a spring of clear water, she could build a hut to replace the cottage—but likely the horsemen would come to burn her in her turn, thinking she was another woodwife. Or she could go to the village, and perhaps someone would be brave enough to take her in—but within a year the lord would be sending for her, exercising his claim on the maidenhead of every lass in his domain. And then she would be wed to whatever man the lord chose for her, whether she liked it or not. And for the rest of her life she would belong to the man, his chattel to labor for him, just as his cow and his ox were his chattel.

And those were the only perchances for her, assuming that she did not really wish to become a privy cleaner or a chimney sweep or a beggar wandering the commons and byways.

Except—

There was one more thing she might do—a perchance so chancy, so secret, so much a dream, that she only let the thought flicker for a moment before she snuffed it out as if it burned. But the thought returned and took the form of two perilous words, and they kept coming back, a little longer each time:

My father.

For a long while she sat. The sun had slipped far down the sky and the shadows had lengthened before she stirred.

Stiffly she got up. Beside her stood her basket, half filled with the coltsfoot she had gathered that morning, when she had been young and carefree. She picked it up and walked forward into the ashes. They had cooled enough so that they did not burn her bare, tough feet if she picked her way, taking care not to step on embers. Keeping to the thin, whitening ash, she ventured past what was left of the cottage walls, then saw what she was looking for: a charred human form.

When she saw the body, Rosemary felt her legs turn to wood so that she stood still. She felt her throat close and the grief in her chest swell till she could barely breathe, till her sorrow grew larger than she was, far larger, sorrow in the forest shadows, sorrow in the setting sun.

The blackened body lay serene and arrow-straight, arms folded over the chest. It could be no one else but Celandine. Just from looking, Ro could tell how it had gone: the helmeted riders, the threats, the torches put to the thatch, and——Celandine standing under the flames, calm and defiant, sending the potent spell of protection upon her daughter. Then, unable to breathe from the smoke, Celandine had laid herself down beside the hearth to die.

She guarded my life.

And gave her own.

Rosemary swallowed hard and felt her chest heaving, yet still she could not weep. Instead, she reached into her basket, took coltsfoot and scattered it on the body. Yellow blossoms, as yellow as celandine flowers. A goodly plant, coltsfoot, the first bright flower of spring, the dried head good for tinder, the whole green plant or the dried leaves good for boiling into a healing tea. A fitting tribute to Celandine.

Yellow flowers shone fairer than gold on the black ashes. And something else shone. Silver.

Ro stooped and picked it up: her mother's gimmal ring.

How had it survived the fire? It should have melted into a lump, yet there it lay, cool and sweetwater clean, in her hand. Its intertwined strands of precious metal had loosened and fallen apart; Ro stood and puzzled them back together. There. The band made of many bands lay whole and well in the cup of her palm. She embraced it with her fingers, then slipped it into her apron pocket.

She bent and started piling blackened stones and charred timbers into a cairn over her mother's body.

By the time she had finished, full dark had fallen and the wolves were singing. Rosemary no longer feared them. She did not even fear the decision she had to make.

The decision she had already made. She was the daughter of a woman who had lived free, serving all yet serving no man. Ro's blood ran as free as a forest stream. She knew she could not spend her life toiling in some lord's cabbage patch. She had to go where her mother's memory led her.

She took one last look at what had been her home, then turned and walked away.

Two

She walked to the edge of the glade where she had lived all her life.

Twilight was darkening to nightfall under the trees, but her bare feet knew the way to the spring. Mama would have found the way even in the darkest dark of the moon by feeling the tug of the sweetwater in her body. She had tried to teach this power, the simplest of woodsy magics, to Rosemary, but Ro could not learn. Not that, or the ways of finding metal, or sending calls and protections, or understanding the news in the wind. Something in Rosemary could not absorb the woodwife's ancient arts. "I am not worthy to be called your daughter," she had said to her mother once, and Mama had hugged her and told her it did not matter. As it truly did not—not to Mother.

Ro could see the spring now. Down in the hollow the water shimmered.

It flowed out from under the roots of a massive oak and trickled down amid ferns and into a stone-lined pool. Ro crouched and whispered, "By your leave, spirit." She had never seen the spirit of the spring, but she knew it was there; anyone with sense could tell that there was life in water, just as there was life in fire and earth and air. Water sang and chuckled and roared. Water ran and leapt and wept and slept. It was the life in water that passed into green growing things and the red deer and the fallow deer and all creatures, including her. After she had acknowledged the spirit, she put her mouth to the surface of the pool and drank, wondering when she would again taste the sweetwater of Celandine's spring.

"I will come back," she whispered to the water. "I will come back someday, and I will find out the names of those who set their torches to the thatch, and they will pay. Somehow they will pay."

When she had grown old enough, strong enough, wise enough to make it happen.

After she had drunk, she murmured an apology to the spirit and washed the soot from her hands and feet. She took the gimmal ring from her apron pocket and placed it on her finger. Then she pulled off her apron and frock, twisted them into a loose rope and hung it around her neck. Dressed only in her small-clothes, she started to climb the oak.

It was a huge, ancient oak, greater around than four men could span with their arms, but it offered some low gnarls for footholds. Often Rosemary had bundled her skirts above her knees and climbed it. Her hands and her bare feet knew the way.

Far above the ground she came to her secret place, the treetrunk hollow where she kept a few things of which her mother knew nothing. Or, if Celandine knew, of which she had never spoken.

She'll never speak again. She's dead.

And so is my heart.

Dry-eyed, sitting on a bough almost as broad as a bench, Ro reached into the hollow oak and pulled out a bow and a sheaf of arrows.

"He's going to laugh at you," she told the bow. She had made it herself out of a young yew tree, with great labor, but it was a poor thing, and she knew it. The arrows were poor things with no tips except the sharpened birch wood.

"Toads take it," she grumbled, a phrase of which her mother had not approved, although it was better than swearing by Deus or the Lady. "He's going to laugh himself silly."

She did not dare to actually speak the words *my father,* but the thought of them made her dead heart come back to life for a moment and beat like lark wings rising.

She had never met him. He was an outlaw, her mother had told her, a wolf's-head: one who could be killed by anyone for a reward of two hundred pounds, just as a wolf could be killed for bounty. He lived the life of a wolf, too, out in the cold and the rain with nothing but a thorn thicket for covering, and he preyed on lords and clerks and rich travelers. Many such outlaws turned savage, but her father was different, her mother had said. He was generous to poor folk and gentle to women and children. Still, he kept around him a band of desperate men. An outlaw camp was not a fitting place for a woman to venture.

Rosemary tucked her frock and apron into the tree hollow, then pulled out a rough wool jerkin she had bartered from the shepherd boy who grazed his flock at the edge of the forest. "Good thing I don't have bosoms," she muttered as she pulled on the jerkin; it covered her almost to her knees. Some of the village girls her age had bosoms already and teased her because she had none. "I don't want any," Ro told the tree. "I don't want that monthly messiness, either." For all she cared, her hips could stay narrow and her body arrow-straight for the rest of her life.

Her hands searched the hollow again and found a spare bowstring. Carefully she took the gimmal ring from her finger, threaded it onto the string, tied the ends behind her neck and hid the string and the ring under her jerkin.

An outlaw camp was not a fitting place for a girl to venture, either.

Perhaps there was no need to be so cautious. He was said to be a generous outlaw. But Rosemary did not know—the minstrels sang of him, but what was he like, really, this stranger, her father? He had never come to see her, never sent word to her, never—never anything. Why?

Was it because he did not want her?

Was it because she was a girl?

She fumbled for her apron and found the knife in its pocket. Because she had no hose to go under the jerkin, she cut her brown frock crosswise in the middle, then slit the bottom part in front and back.

Bound around her waist under the jerkin, it would serve as leggings. She cut long ribbons of cloth for the crisscross wrappings she would need.

There was one more thing she had to do.

With her knife in one hand, she pulled her hair taut with the other and hacked it off. Long, brown tresses fell away, and she threw them into the tree hollow. People sheared their hair when they were grieving, didn't they? It felt right. When she finished, her head felt light and cool. Her hair formed a rough stubble around her ears, as if she were a peasant boy.

When she had made the bow and arrows, when she had bartered for the jerkin, she had told herself that it was a game. She liked to pretend to be a boy sometimes.

But it wasn't a game any longer. To go where a girl could not venture, she would travel as a boy.

It would be a long journey. The famous outlaw who was her father roamed Sherwood Forest most of the time, but wandered seldom to Barnesdale, or to the smaller forests north of Barnesdale, such as Celandine's Wood.

With her bow and arrows slung over her back and her knife and leggings tied around her waist, Rosemary shinnied down the oak, leaving what little was left of her old life in the hollow.

"Good-bye, oak," she whispered. "Good-bye, spring."

Her heart throbbed like larksong. She was going to find him. She would meet him at last. Her father, Robin Hood.

Three

A few nightfalls later, Rosemary sat by a small campfire in Barnesdale Forest, trying to cook rabbit stew. For want of a pot, she was steaming the meat, mushrooms, greens and a few wild onions in the rabbit skin stretched over the fire upon four sticks stuck in the ground. The hair was scorching off the rabbit hide. "Go ahead," she told it. "Burn through. Dump my supper in the fire. Toads take it." She sat in a damp hollow, her feet almost raw enough to bleed, her face and arms stung by nettles and scratched by thorns, her legs sore from climbing all day over boulders and deadfalls, her arms and shoulders aching from waiting with drawn bow to shoot her supper, her wrist burning from the snap of the bowstring, her fingers sore in like wise, almost every part of her as sore as her heart. She hadn't eaten much since—since what had happened to her mother. She knew she needed to eat, and she was cooking the stew in an attempt to make herself eat, but in her heart she did not much care whether she lived or died.

She hunched close to the fire, for the night was cold and felt like rain. "Go ahead," she mumbled to the night, "rain on me." When you're sleeping on rocks and roots with not even a shawl for covering, what's a little rain? Somewhere deep in the forest, wolves howled at the waning moon. "Go ahead and howl," Rosemary said. "I don't care. I—"

She glanced up and saw green eyes shining beyond her fire.

The sight jolted her to her feet, her heart beating hard as she snatched up her bow. It seemed that she did care after all whether she lived. In the near-darkness she caught a glimpse of pricked ears, white fangs. Wolf! With trembling fingers she fumbled an arrow onto her bowstring. She could not hope to kill a wolf; her wooden-tipped arrows would not kill anything larger than a hare or a partridge. But she hoped to sting it hard enough to drive it away. If not—she did not dare to think what might happen.

She drew her bow and shot at the green-shining eyes.

The moment her arrow flew, Ro knew she had done it all wrong. Instead of leaning into the bow, she had snatched at the string. The arrow was flying short and off to one side.

The green-eyed, white-fanged shadow leapt.

Ro's mouth opened but her scream stopped short as the wolf leapt—and seized the arrow out of the air. Its great jaws snapped shut on the shaft, and it dropped to earth again as lightly as a cat. Just across the fire from her, it stood with the arrow in its mouth and its pink tongue lolling, panting and grinning at her.

Ro gawked.

She had seen wolves. This was a wolf—yet not a wolf. Thickly furred and silver-gray—but with a rift of golden brown across the shoulders and a bib of white on its broad chest, like a shepherd's collie. Big and lean, with strong legs and massive, silent paws— but standing there with its ears pricked toward her and its tail in the air like feathers on a hat, wagging. With her arrow in its mouth.

It took two short bounces toward her and dropped the arrow on the ground. It flattened to its elbows and feinted at the arrow with its teeth. It crouched with its nose to the ground and its rump in the air, tail waving. It pawed at the arrow. It sprang up, bounced sideward and smiled at her with great expectation.

Rosemary felt the inside of her mouth drying out from gaping. She closed it and swallowed. She remembered how to breathe now. Deep breath. Deep. Good. "Toads," she whispered. Despite her aching muscles and her wrist and fingers stinging anew, she put another arrow to her bow. This time she aimed off to one side of the—puppy. This big-pawed, cavorting creature was an overgrown puppy if she'd ever seen one.

A puppy that—that snatched bolts out of the air?

She shot the arrow. It flew high. Her visitor sprang five feet off the ground and landed silently on padded paws, her arrow in its teeth.

"*Lady* toads." Ro crouched. "Bring it here," she coaxed, one hand outstretched.

The wolfish pup padded toward her. She felt her heart pounding. What if—

It wagged its tail and dropped the arrow where she could reach it.

"Good boy," Ro said. "Are you a boy?" Yes, he was. She could see that he was. "You think I'm a boy, too, don't you?"

The pup bounced back, eager to catch another arrow.

"No more right now." Ro folded to the ground, to a lumpy seat on blackthorn roots, feeling a trifle weak. "Toads have mercy. Are you hungry?" Her supper had not dumped on the fire after all. Shakily she managed to retrieve the rabbit skin, holding it by its corners between her hands, waiting for the food to cool a bit before she tried to eat it.

The wolf—or whatever he was—sat by the far side of her campfire with his bushy tail curled around his haunches and his large forepaws side by side. He watched her face, not the food.

He did not act hungry. And he looked sleek enough—she herself probably looked scrawnier. But if he did not want her to feed him, and if he did not want to kill her and gnaw her haunches, then—then what did he want?

Ro dug a hollow in the ground with her heel and set her supper in it. Spearing a mushroom with her knife, she nibbled on it. Her throat tightened against the food, as usual these days, but she made herself eat. And as she ate, she gazed back at the dark eyes studying her from across the fire.

Sober brown eyes. It was only the reflected firelight that had made them look spooksheen-green. Rosemary said to her visitor, "You're like me."

She swallowed onion, potherbs, a bit of meat. It

was easier to eat with someone to talk to. Talking lightened the stone of grief in her chest.

She said, "You don't fit in. You're part dog, aren't you? Part dog and part wolf. So you don't belong anywhere. Not in the forest and not in the village and not in the lord's hall."

She lifted the rabbit skin to her mouth and sipped some broth. She put it down again.

"Well, you're not the only one," she told the wolf-dog softly. "I don't fit in, either. First of all, I'm a girl and I don't want to be. I don't want to be owned by some man. I don't want to spend my life making babies and churning butter. But that's not the worst of it." Rosemary paused at the edge of her secret as if it were a cliff. She had never told anyone. Her mother's strictest rule was that she must never tell.

But her mother was dead. She badly needed to talk to someone. And the wolf-dog would not betray her.

Keeping her voice very low, she said, "I'm part *aelfin*. My mother—her father was human, but her mother was one of the *aelfe,* the old ones under the hollow hills. They drove out my grandmother for loving a human, and they would not accept my mother, either, and the castle folk—" Rosemary swallowed hard, remembering what the men on horses had done. "The castle folk called her a witch."

The wolf-dog stretched out his forelegs and lay down, placidly accepting all this.

"She was very beautiful," Rosemary told him. In her mother, human warmth had blended with the silvery moonlit glow of the aelfe. Rosemary wished she herself were half as beautiful. "She could become a wildflower or a birch tree or a thrush on the wing when the power was strong in her." Likely folk thought that she, Rosemary, had similar powers. Well, they were mistaken. What had woodsy magic done for her mother? Gotten her killed, that was what. "She knew every plant's goodness. She could heal sty, colic, childbed fever. So they called her a witch." Ro stared into her dwindling campfire. The flickering brightness of the flames made her blink.

Deep in his throat the wolf-dog made a small sound almost like a whimper.

"Likely I'll never belong, either," Rosemary muttered, blinking at the fire. "Not even—not even where I'm going." She could not bring herself to speak of her father, because the thought of him made her heart flutter. She did not know which was harder to bear: her fear that he would not accept her or her hope that he would.

She glanced at the food and knew that she could eat no more of it. "Are you hungry?" she asked the wolf-dog.

Head lifted, he gazed at her.

She offered a chunk of meat between her fingers. "Fancy a bite of rabbit?"

The wolf-dog glanced at the tidbit but did not move.

Ro addressed him seriously. "Are you looking for company? Would you like to travel with me?"

He got up then and padded around the fire to her. But he did not take the meat from her hand. Instead, he licked her face.

Four

She named him Tykell, the arrow.

When she lay down by the fire to sleep, Tykell lay by her side. Pressed against his warm fur, with the embers of her campfire at her back, Ro slept with some ease for the first time since she had been wandering. She awoke at dawn only partly soaked by dew and only half frozen.

It had not rained after all. Not yet.

Moving on was simple; she slung her bundle of arrows on her back, picked up her bow in one hand and a skinful of cold rabbit meat in the other, and started to walk in what she hoped was the right direction, a bit south of sunrise. The wolf-dog paced by her side.

"Ty," she told him, "I have too many problems." His company made her feel able to face them. "I need shoes or my feet are going to wear off. I don't have enough to eat. And even if I did, I'd probably shiver it all off at night. I need a better bow and arrows so I can shoot deer. I need a mantle, a blanket, a cooking pot, bread . . ." Rosemary's heart ached at the thought of bread, her mother's light wheat loaves warm from the oven. ". . . bread and butter and eggs and—and a milch cow, I suppose," she added, rolling her eyes, "to follow me around and carry it all."

It was rough wilderness that she walked, not a fitting place for a cow. Great oaks, elms and beeches towered from rocky slopes, throwing the hollows into chill shadow. Ivy and wild grape hung thick on the tree trunks, their tendrils brushing Rosemary's head as she found her way through them. A gray moth fluttered past her face, landed on a rough gray trunk and disappeared at once. A pheasant whirred up, invisible until it took flight. Ferns frothed like a green torrent over and between the rocks. Eat fern seed, folk said, and one could be invisible, like the wild things—but one could spend one's whole life searching for fern seed. Or fern flower—Mother had said that the eating of fern flower had the power to make folk immortal. Like the aelfe. Rosemary felt her skin prickle at the thought of the ancient ones, her kin, hidden in the forest all around her.

"I'm giving myself goose bumps," she told Tykell.

Did men who were outlawed feel this way about the forest, she wondered, or did they grow to hate it? She was beginning to understand what it meant to be an outlaw. It was more than just being hunted like a wolf. It was also going without—without warmth, home, hearth, a roof overhead—where was an outlaw to go when it rained? Or in the freezing winter? When the snow blew three feet deep?

She did not know the answers.

All around her the forest breathed and listened and waited. Leaves flickered although there was no breeze. The ferns stirred as earth exhaled, leaving upon them drops of dew. From the dank hollows, mists rose, coiling up like smoke.

A roe deer sprang out of nowhere. Ro stood still to watch it leap away, but Tykell gave a single loud bark and dashed after it.

"Ty!" Ro cried.

Bounding up a jumbled hillside behind the deer, the wolf-dog seemed not to hear her.

"Tykell!"

He disappeared over the hilltop.

Ro ran after him. She knew she could not catch him, she knew it would have made better sense to wait for him where he had left her, but her pounding heart made her run anyway. Crashing through vines and bracken, struggling over deadfalls, she panted as sweat ran into her eyes, making them sting. She scraped her arms on brush, cut her feet bloody on the rocks, blundered on. The hill rose so steep that she had to cling to saplings to haul herself to the top. Standing on the crest, she gasped for breath, looking all around.

She saw mist rising, gray breath of earth, and the green mist of new leaves. Nothing more. As her breathing quieted, she listened. She heard only birds.

She drew a long breath, then called. "Ty-kell!"

She waited. Called again. Waited some more.

Nothing.

"Oh, toads take it!"

Where was he, the muttonhead? Would she ever be able to find him?

No. Likely not, half-wild thing that he was. He had been her companion for half a day, then left her.

Now Ro could no longer say that it was only sweat making her eyes sting. But she tightened her face against the tears.

"Fool dog," she whispered.

Lips pressed together, she glanced at the sun, blinking. Then she turned to the south and east, toward Sherwood Forest, and trudged on.

"Toads, what's this?" Ro murmured, peering through a thicket of wild quince. Beyond the bushes, a rift in the trees let sunlight flood in to puddle golden on soft turf. Ro stared at a grassy track, a path too plain to have been made by deer, winding through the forest.

"Hard to tell, but it seems to head the right way . . ."

She looked and listened for any hint of danger, then wormed her way through the bushes to walk on the path. Oh, blessed ease, to walk so freely, even though the track was barely wide enough for two men to pass each other. Meandering like a stream, it found a way for Rosemary between steep hillsides and giant oaks and great stones, and yes, it seemed to tend mostly south and east, toward Sherwood, still many days' travel away. Sunshine warmed Rosemary's shoulders and new leaves brushed her cheeks as she limped along. Violets, buttercups and primroses grew in the soft new grass that eased her sore feet as the brightness of the blossoms eased her sore heart.

Eyes on the flowers as she rounded the next curve of the path, Rosemary heard a sniffling sound. Some animal? No, but up until now she had not met with a human soul, so it took her a moment to realize: someone with a stuffy nose.

A beggar, a brigand, or some lord's warden? Danger? She jerked her head up, staring.

Then her mouth opened in a manner that she knew to be uncouth.

Sitting amid primroses along the side of the path, a very large person twirled a single butter-colored blossom between his fingers.

Even sitting down, he was almost as tall as Ro. His broad shoulders and deep chest filled out his primrose-yellow jerkin, but on those strong-looking shoulders curled girlish tresses of fawn-colored hair. His sturdy legs, in sky-blue hose, sprawled across the path, and his feet, each of which looked as big as a horse's head, pointed skyward in red leather shoes with long tips that curled up like fern fronds. He wore a short red cape and a red pointed hat with a tuft of quail feathers on the side, and under the hat he turned to Rosemary a face rose-petal soft and smooth.

"Oh!" he shrieked at her. "Oh! Who are you? Don't hurt me!"

Ro felt her jaw sag even worse at this greeting. "For the love of heaven, why would I hurt you?" She stared at the stranger—the boy. His height made her want to see him as a man, but his soft, hairless face and something loose-limbed and coltish about him told her that he was younger than his size made him seem. His face looked as bland as a baby's, his curling locks baby-fine, and his mouth, softly steepled like a baby's mouth, quivered with distress. "What's the matter?" Ro asked him.

"Oh! It's that dreadful man. I am all a mass of nerves," he said in a quick, husky voice.

"What dreadful man?"

"The horse man." He held the primrose to his nose and breathed deeply, as if it were a perfumed handkerchief to keep foul odors away from him. "Dreadful. A most unpleasant person."

A knight, Rosemary thought, or a lord, or some lord's man-at-arms. Some man on horseback. She would do well to be wary of anyone on horseback. "What did he do to you?"

"He *shouted* at me. All I did was ask him for a farthing or a lump of cheese or what you will, and he *roared* at me and told me to get out of his way."

That didn't sound so bad. "And did you?"

"Well, of course!" The primrose boy's soft mouth trembled. "My dear little lad, have you by chance a bit of food about you? I feel weak."

"I'm not your dear little lad!" Rosemary said before she remembered that she was, indeed, a lad, and certainly she was little by comparison with him. "You're no older than I am," she added.

"Be a dear fellow, just the same. Have you something to eat? I would be most grateful."

Ro could not believe it. This well-padded lunk begging from her? When she was standing there in a patched jerkin and ragged brown leggings while he sat at ease in his fine gaudy clothes with three big bags, yellow and blue and red, bulging like onions in the grass by his side, and what could he have in those bags except food or money? Any real outlaw, Ro knew, would have taken those bags away from him and probably would have pulled the fine clothes off of him as well. But he looked at her with such puppy-dog eyes that she could not help but smile at him.

"Here." She untied the skin full of cold rabbit meat from the strip of cloth she wore by way of belt. She was homeless, wandering, footsore, Tykell had run away, and who cared anymore if she was starving? She just wanted to lie down and die anyway— what did some cold meat matter? She handed it over.

The boy took it with a gasp of gratitude. "Thank you, my dear fellow."

"Eat it in good health." Ro turned to go on her way.

"Wait, my dear lad. I must give you something in return," he said, and he handed her his primrose.

Five

It occurred to Rosemary as she trudged on that she should have asked the large boy which way the horseman went. But it did not matter. She had walked almost a league since she had left the primrose boy, and the horseman was most likely traveling twice as fast. He should be well ahead of her by now—

Ro heard a clatter of hooves. Her head jerked up. She gasped and clutched at her bow.

Coming at her from around the next curve in the path, at a ramping gait fit to run her down, loomed a foaming black warhorse with—with two heads?

"Step aside," ordered a harsh voice.

Ro had already stepped aside, so startled that it took her several beats of her pounding heart to see what the primrose boy had meant when he had said "horse man": The black steed's second head was a rider armored in black horsehide. Ears, mane and all, horsehide mantled him, and what had been the skin of the horse's head rode on his head like a visored helm, hiding his face. He peered out through an eye-slit. Rosemary could see only his cleft chin and his thin, hard mouth as he rode past her—

He jerked his steed to a halt. "You go armed, boy?" he barked at her.

Ro took another step back. Robin Hood would not have stepped back or stepped aside, she knew. Robin Hood or any proper outlaw would have said, *I have as much right to go armed as you do, I have as much right to the path as you.* Robin would have pulled this bully off his high horse and fought him in an eyeblink. But he scared her so badly that she could not speak, could not think what he wanted of her.

"Arrows!" he roared. "Arrows and bow!"

Her so-called bow, her poor wooden-tipped arrows—he took exception to them for some reason? Ro managed to say, "What—what's wrong with them?"

"Those are outlaw weapons," he snapped. "I am Guy of Gisborn. I hunt outlaws."

She blinked at him, beginning to understand. He was patrolling; that was why she had met him head-on when she expected him to be traveling ahead of her.

35

"Give them here." He held out a hand sheathed in black leather.

Her bow, her arrows—he wanted to take them away from her. She did not move.

"Hand them over!"

All the while he spoke, he curbed his lathered steed with one black-gloved fist on the reins. If it did not obey him, perhaps he would kill it to wear its skin on his head and body? The horse jigged in place, sweat frothing white on its slick black neck, its frightened eyes glinting white.

"Hand me your weapons, sirrah," Guy of Gisborn said, his growl eloquent of danger, "and perhaps I will not give you the thrashing you deserve."

But—no. She couldn't. She shook her head. "I need them." Her bow and arrows could shoot only birds and rabbits, but without them, she would surely starve.

Guy of Gisborn pulled hard on the reins, yanking his horse into a low rear. "You need the flat of my blade across your back, churl!" he roared, his hand on his sword hilt.

Ro had not meant her words as defiance, but now she found that there was defiance in her after all. The overgrown bully, who did he think he was? If he wanted her poor weapons so much, let him come and get them. With her fist tightening on her bow, she turned and walked on her way.

Guy of Gisborn bellowed like a charging boar. He swung his horse to run her down. She dodged toward the edge of the track, thick with blackthorn—but from the thorns rose a wolfish growl, a roar as loud as the outlaw-hunter's. Out of the brush sprang Tykell.

"Ty!" Rosemary gasped, almost dropping her bow.

Fangs bared, Tykell leapt past Ro and lunged at the horseman's booted leg.

Then it was all a blur of stormwind roar, Ro's pulse roaring in her ears and Ty snarling and Gisborn yelling as he drew his sword, and a scream—her own—but even louder she heard the black charger shrill with terror. And with the tip of her bow against her instep she was tugging the string into place, and it was all happening at once, Gisborn swinging his booted foot at Tykell and flailing with his sword, Ty leaping aside then lunging again, the wild-eyed horse plunging away from the wolf-dog—

The steed shrilled again and reared over Tykell so high its black underbelly loomed. "Ty, watch out!" Ro cried as she snatched an arrow from her sheaf. But then she saw a gray flurry as Tykell darted aside, and a silvery flash as Gisborn's sword dropped, thudding to the ground. The outlaw hunter had to cling to his horse's mane with both hands to stay on.

In one quick movement Ro nocked her arrow to the string and drew the bow.

Guy of Gisborn righted himself and his horse, facing her. His sword lay in the grass. Tykell stood just in front of Rosemary, snarling. Ro stood with all her body's weight bending the horns of her bow, arrow pointed straight at Guy of Gisborn's face. Her wooden-tipped arrow could not possibly penetrate his leather armor, but if it found his eyeslit, it could tidily pierce his eye.

She did not speak. She did not need to.

For a moment, except for the mutter of Ty's growling, all was profoundly still.

"I will remember you, boy," Guy of Gisborn yelled. "Watch your step. I will be looking for you." Letting his sword lie where it was, he wheeled his horse away. "If it were not that I have more important things to do, I would kill you today." He sent the steed ramping off. Rosemary watched as he rode away, his shaggy black mane-of-a-dead-horse flying behind him.

Rosemary breathed out.

"Oh, Ty," she whispered, and she went down on

her knees, her arms around the wolf-dog's neck as he wagged and panted and grinned at her. Now that Gisborn was gone, she felt herself trembling like water. "Oh, Ty. You idiot." She ran her hands over him, feeling for injuries. No blood. No bruising. He seemed all right. She hugged him again and laid her face in the comfort of his fur. "You fleabrain, where have you been?"

Her heart felt as light as a butterfly. It was all right. It was all right now. Ty had come back to her.

As the shadows lengthened toward evening, Ro left the grassy path and walked quietly among the trees with her bow at the ready and an arrow nocked, on the hunt for supper.

She had walked far that day, and had eaten nothing but raw greens, lambs' lettuce and such. For a while she had lugged Guy of Gisborn's sword with her, thinking she might use it for chopping firewood, but then it had seemed just too heavy, and she had dropped it in the bracken. And she felt even weaker now. Her hands shook with hunger, and she began to feel a soundless buzz of panic behind her eyes.

Tykell's head came up as he looked at something, and then Ro saw also: On the limb of an oak, a big fox squirrel lay sunning itself. Flat on its belly with its legs out to the sides, it looked funny, like an auburn wig perched there—but Ro was too hungry to smile. It was lying still, that was all she cared about. The forest was never going to give her a better shot. She leaned into the bow, steady, steady, taking aim—

Just as the bowstring sang, Ty leapt and snatched her arrow out of the air. "Ty!" Ro yelled. "You curdlehead!" The squirrel jumped up, scolding, and darted away behind the trunk of the oak. Ro folded to the ground, too tired to cry. "Oh, Ty!"

His wagging tail slowed down, and he whined, his ears uncertain. He dropped the arrow close to her, gave a small bounce and pawed at it, trying to get her to play.

"No. Ty, listen. Catch arrows if somebody shoots them at you. Not when I'm trying to shoot us some dinner."

Talking was no use, of course. Ro cradled his head between her hands, caressing the ruff of gray fur at each side of his face, gazing into his puzzled brown eyes and considering the perchances. Tie him to a tree while she went hunting? But he would not stand for it—he was a free, wild thing, staying with her by his own choice. If she tied him, he would chew through the tether in two snaps, go away and never come back. Let him go away? Or make him go away, drive him away? For one flickering instant Ro thought of shouting, striking, throwing stones, and then she shuddered and closed her eyes. No. She could not do that to Ty. She would starve first.

As seemed more and more likely. She stared at Ty, baffled. "Lard-for-brains," she appealed to him, "what am I going to do?"

Six

Rosemary could not sleep. She lay in a warm, dry nest of bracken, but the ache of hunger kept her awake. That, and the ache in her heart. Ty had gone off in the dark somewhere. She wished she could hunt while he was gone. But she was not half wolf, fit to hunt at night in only the light of a crescent moon.

Sherwood Forest lay two weeks ahead of her, she judged. Longer if she walked slowly. And if she could not walk at all, if she starved . . .

She clenched her teeth, biting back the thought. She must get there.

But how was she to survive?

She looked up into darkness as soft as moleskin. A

breeze whispered in the trees, brushed her cheek, gentle as a mother. But it gave her no answer.

A waft of sound drifted to her on the cool green-scented breeze.

Rosemary sat up, holding her breath to hear that sweet yearning murmur, wondering whether she had been dreaming. That must have been it. But no, there it was again, a whisper of music as quicksilver dewy as the night. Rosemary gasped and startled to her feet. That echo on the wind called to her, tugged her like the bowstring of her heart. Without a thought for anything else she lunged into the night, following that wisp of sound.

With only moonlight to help her she blundered through the forest, sore feet treading on rocks and sticks in the darkness. It was coming to her more clearly now, the gossamer song. Behind a golden thread of melody she could hear the silver weave of harp strings. But it was the voice of the singer that drew her. His voice: as if windflowers could sing, as if bluebells could ring. He sang like stormwind, like dancing water, like wild honey flowing. Rosemary had heard her mother humming in the cottage, harvesters chanting in the fields, a shepherd lad piping on a willow flute, but she had never heard such music as this. Now she was near enough to understand the words:

"Alas, my love, you do me wrong
To cast me off discourteously,
For I have loved you so long
Delighting in your company.
Greensleeves was all my joy
And Greensleeves was my delight,
Greensleeves was my heart of gold . . ."

Who could it be, this golden-voiced minstrel? Rosemary felt her way closer—

Then she saw. There he sat in the heart of a beech grove, on a bed made of fir tips, with a blanket folded beside him and a campfire at his feet and his three pouches in a row beside him. There he sat cradling his harp to his chest and lifting his face to the night and singing.

It was the boy who had given her a primrose.

Standing back from the light of his fire so as not to interrupt the song, Ro listened, gawking. Who would have believed that such a soaring butterfly voice could come out of such an oafish body? Yet there he sat with his long, curling hair catching the moonlight, with his eyes half lidded and his soft mouth parted in song. And what he sang made her heart beat faster:

"In hidden glades of wild Sherwood
 There lives an archer fair and free,
 An outlaw bold as gold, yet good
 Of heart. Folk call him Robin Hood . . ."

Then Ro saw——she was not the only one listening. In that moment she could hear nothing but the pounding of her own heartbeat. For that moment she stopped breathing.

At first she had thought it was only the firelight shimmering on the silvery trunks of the beeches. But——the light had faces.

Faces as still and shining as deep water, faces never roughened by winter's wind or summer's sweat or rash or pox or any mortal troubles. Faces that glowed like silver candlelight. Faces warlike and bold, or shy and maidenly, or seeress serene, or quiet, or glad, or fierce, or gently sad——ancient faces, but never old. Rosemary could not think of them as old. These were the ageless ones, the aelfe.

Her kin.

Even though they manifested only dimly as faint human-sized lights floating amid the trees, Ro's knees weakened at the sight of them. She hugged herself and folded to the ground. The spell of the music would not let her leave. Yet her awe of the aelfe would not let her draw any nearer.

The primrose boy was singing of Robin Hood wearing ragged red clothes and going to Nottingham and winning the golden arrow at the contest by which the sheriff meant to snare him. There were many such ballads of Robin Hood, telling how he went forth from Sherwood as a wandering friar or a tinker or a beggar or a potter who sold his wares at the sheriff's door and kissed the sheriff's wife. Whenever she had heard such tales, Ro had thought how very stupid the sheriff must be not to know Robin Hood when he saw him, no matter what clothing Robin wore. But this time, listening as the boy-minstrel sang to the midnight forest, she held no such thoughts. The spell of the music took her away from herself. She no longer felt her aching belly or her aching heart. She barely knew where she was, who she was. So rapt that she barely breathed, she listened.

At the end of the song, the harper boy drew breath, and Rosemary listened to silence as deep as the night, with not even a leaf rustling. The boy lowered his head, opened his eyes, then blinked. For the first time he seemed aware of his listeners, although not surprised. He gave the aelfe a shy smile, then lifted his head again, closed his eyes, strummed his harp and sang on.

He sang of a young woman who died for love and was transformed into a swan. He sang of Robin Hood robbing a rich burgher and giving the gold to the poor. He sang of King Arthur, and of Tam Lin, and of Robin Hood again. He sang of two faithful lovers killed, and buried side by side, and how roses grew up and embraced over their graves.

Then he bowed his head and set his harp aside.

Rosemary took a long breath. All of the forest seemed to breathe. A breeze sighed, leaves whispered. Somewhere an owl cried. The moon, a white bow in the ink-blue sky, had dipped low.

The presences of the aelfe shimmered among the beeches, and a deep voice spoke. "Beg of us a boon, harper."

Ro pulled her knees to her chest, making herself very small. She could not tell which old one had spoken; that low, commanding voice seemed to come from the earth itself.

The harper gazed like a wide-eyed child. "A boon?" he said. "Oh, my dear fellow, I thank you. But I need no boon." He reached out to touch his harp with his fingertips. "I have everything I need."

"You are blessed among mortals, then." The voice

was very gentle. "But think, harper. Is there no boon we can grant you?"

"Truly, no. I am content." The harper boy heaved himself up and shambled to his feet—he stood nearly seven feet tall. "Yon dear little lad was kind to me today," he added, pointing with his chin toward Rosemary. "Could you grant him a boon instead of me?"

Ro froze like a rabbit in a thicket. She had not thought that the minstrel boy knew she was there.

He bowed deeply. "You'll excuse me, my dear listeners? I am only a humble mortal, and I must obey the needs of my body." He ambled off into the woods.

"Would you care to beg a boon, yon dear little lad?" The deep aelfin voice resonated with what might have been mockery or mirth.

At first Rosemary's mind would not work at all, and then too many thoughts flew in at once, like a swarm of grasshoppers. Should she make herself known to the aelfe as their kin? No, she didn't dare. Could she accept a boon from them? There were so many things she needed: clothing, shoes, a blanket, food—

"Ask of us a boon, little one." No mirth in the voice now, but maybe an edge of impatience.

Clothes shoes food blanket money . . .

But—something in Ro did not want to be a beggar. "Speak, youngster."

Rosemary straightened and spoke, at first in a whisper, then more clearly. "I am very hungry," she said, "but I do not want you to give me food. If you really wish to help me, then please let me find a way to help myself. Feed myself."

The aelfin voice echoed around her again, once more with a quirk of mirth in it. "Use the gifts your mother gave you, daughter of Celandine."

Rosemary gasped, then bolted to her feet, staring to see which face had spoken.

But there was nothing there. No one. The aelfin glow had flickered away. She saw only tricky moonlight, silver beeches, a harp sitting upon the ground. She heard only the soft breathing of earth and air and trees.

She turned and stumbled back to her camp in a daze.

Tykell lay there, placidly panting. On the ground by his forepaws lay a very mangled dead rabbit.

Ro went down on her knees and hugged him. "Okay," she told him, "I'd rather shoot my own supper, but thanks." She gathered twigs to start a fire and cook herself a very late dinner. She knew she was not going to be able to sleep. Too much had happened. The minstrel. The aelfe. How had they known who she was? And—were they laughing at her? Did they despise her? They had given her no boon.

Or so she thought at first. But as she whispered a by-your-leave to the spirit of fire and struck flint against the steel blade of her knife, as sparks leapt into her kindling and small flames licked up, she saw the firelight glow on her bow lying near at hand—

Her eyes widened. She reached for the bow.

It was no longer the rude thing she had made for herself. Straight and true, its polished yew shone. Ram's horns tipped the ends to better hold the string of tough braided horsehair coated with yellow beeswax. Ro stood up, placed the tip of the bow against her instep, strung it and drew the string. The bow was right for her. Not a man's longbow, but a boy's bow, strong, but small and light. And the arrows—

Ro barely dared to pick them up, but she did so. In a glossy leather quiver with a pouch on one side— there must have been three dozen arrows. Short arrows, not the clothyard shafts most outlaws used, but birch, balanced and straight and true, fletched with—was that truly peacock? Ro drew one out with shaky fingers. Yes, fletched with peacock feathers that glinted green-gold in the firelight. And tipped, not with steel, but with razor-sharp flint.

"Well," Rosemary whispered. Gently she slid the arrow back into the quiver and put it down. With more need than grace, she sat on the ground. "Toads have mercy," she murmured, and then she raised her head and lifted her voice to the benighted forest. "Thank you, wherever you are," she called softly.

Only the rustling of leaves answered her.

She breathed out. She touched the arrows again, stroking a winking eye of peacock plume with one careful fingertip. "By my poor starved body," she said softly to Tykell, "I am honored. But I am half afraid to use them."

She had never seen such arrows, but she had heard of them. The short, flint-tipped arrows of the old ones. Elf-bolts, folk called them.

Seven

The tall oaks of Sherwood Forest were just opening into sunny green leaf when Rosemary
walked under them a few weeks later. She had shot
deer as she needed them on her journey, and she wore
shoes made of the uncured deerskin with the hair side
turned in, stitched with the sturdy needle she had
found in the pocket of her quiver. In the same way, she
had stitched herself a crude leather belt with a sheath
for her knife, and a leather band to protect her wrist
from the bowstring. Slung over her shoulders were
her bow, her quiver of elf-bolts, and a deerskin pouch
for carrying things she had gathered along the way:
comfrey leaves for healing, willow bark for toothache,
the roots of wake-robin for food when all else failed,
coltsfoot, leeks, feverfew, many herbs for healing and
strengthening. Use the gifts her mother had given her,

the aelfe had said? Perhaps they had meant Celandine's knowledge of plants and herbs. Perhaps not. Rosemary was not sure what they had meant.

She was not sure, either, where in this great forest she might find her father.

She walked along a stream as Tykell romped ahead of her, leaping over rocks and ivy tangles and mossy logs like a deer. Any real deer within bowshot were surely chased away by his antics. But when it came time to hunt, Ro had only to fit an elf-bolt to her bow and Ty would sober and pace by her side. He would not snatch the flint-tipped arrows out of the air. He would not touch them even when they lay on the ground. He did not seem to fear them, yet he would not lay his jaws upon them. Ro had made a few rude wood-tipped arrows to shoot just for Ty, so that he could leap and snatch them and fetch them to her.

The streambank frothed with bluebells, white wild strawberry blossoms and purple columbine cascading over bright, velvety springtime grass. Flowers, stream, forest, all were so lovely that for a moment Rosemary stood beside the trunk of a great-girthed oak and just looked. And listened. Overhead a warbler sang. A sense of peace seeped into Ro. Heart's ease—there was a flower named heartsease, and someday she would find herself some. She missed her

mother—maybe she would always miss Celandine—
but the pain of those first awful days was gone. She
could take care of herself now. Already she had traveled far and learned much. And she had Ty.

Here he came, charging toward her, his great jaws
agape with the sheer panting joy of running, pink
tongue lolling, every white fang shining—

ZING. Something buzzed past Ro's head and
darted straight toward Ty faster than a bird could
fly. But Tykell was even faster. Before Ro could shout
a warning, Ty leapt, turned in midair, snapped and
came down with a goose-fletched clothyard shaft in
his jaws. Ro spun with a yell, so angry that she did
not think to be afraid.

"Stop it!" In two quick motions she strung her bow
and nocked a flint-tipped arrow—she had not known
she could do it so quickly. She leaned into her bow and
aimed toward the man even before she properly saw
him. "Idiot, what do you think you're doing?"

She saw him now and righted her aim. Through a
tangle of ivy, an astonished face looked back at her.
"I wasn't shooting at you," he said. "I was shooting
at the wolf."

"That's my *dog!*"

"Hold your bolt." He stepped out from behind the
ivy, and she could see now why it had been hard to

see him before. He was all dressed in Lincoln green: cap, tunic, and hose, everything oak green except for his low brown leather boots and a leather baldric that held his quiver of clothyard arrows, a short sword and a coiled silver horn such as huntsmen use. He carried a heavy oak staff and a longbow, holding the bow slack in his hand as he walked toward her. "It looks like a wolf," he said. "I thought it had you at bay. I thought it was about to rip you limb from limb." He had a quirky mouth that seemed to make merry of everything, even of himself, as he spoke. Especially of himself.

"By my lady, that so-called dog sniggled my shaft right out of the air," he said, his blue eyes alight with easy wonder, his gaze all for Tykell, not at all for the flint arrowhead still aimed at his chest. He was a tall man, though no taller than many other men, and quick on his feet, with no lankiness about him. He seemed young, but that might have been because he wore no beard—his laughing eyes did not seem so very young. He was tanned by weather, and his tawny skin made the fair hair curling out from under his cap seem all the more golden. He carried his head high. No lord's ploughman, this one. Ro knew that she was looking upon an outlaw. Judging by the Lincoln green he wore, one of Robin Hood's men.

Though she did not shift her stare from the stranger, Rosemary was aware of Tykell standing by her side, dropping the outlaw's arrow at her feet. Panting happily. As the man in green approached, Ty walked forward to meet him, wagging his tail. Ro remembered how Ty had attacked Guy of Gisborn— Ty knew this man meant her no harm. It was as he had said; he had been trying to save her life. She breathed out, blowing away her anger, and lowered her bow.

"Certainly you're not a wolf," said the man to Tykell, round-eyed. "You're a *dog*. I can see that now. Just the same, you'll excuse me if I don't pat you?" He smiled at Ty, then nodded and walked past Ty to stand facing Rosemary. "Would it be presuming too much to ask for my arrow back again?"

She stooped and picked up the arrow, noting its honed steel tip, its straight-grained, balanced shaft, feathered with gray-goose wing pinions. She handed it back to the man in green.

"Thank you." He placed it in his quiver, then put the tip of his bow to the ground to stand and talk. "Where are you going, lad?"

"I'm not a lad," she said, too late realizing that, once more, she should have let it go. What was she, standing there in her dirty jerkin and ragged leggings, if not a lad? But Ro found herself prickly with this man because he had frightened her.

"You're not a lad?" He smiled, his flaxen eyebrows raised, bright on his tanned face. "What are you, then?"

"An outlaw," she said boldly, making the best of her blunder, "and I am on my way to join Robin Hood's band."

"Are you!" He studied her, and she stood and let him look. There was nothing harsh in his stare, no more than if a badger were peering at her out of its burrow. "You carry a fine bow," he said after he had scanned her up and down. "Did you make it?"

"No. Someone gave it to me."

"Oh?" He looked at her some more. "Arrows fletched with peacock, no less!"

"A gift. With the bow." On impulse, she pulled an arrow out of her quiver and handed it to him. "Do you want one? They're too fancy for me."

The man in green leaned his oaken staff against his shoulder and held the elf-bolt in both hands, turning it over and over, squinting at it. Rosemary liked his hands, strong and weathered yet clean-looking, like his face. "Tipped with flint, by my poor old eyes," he murmured. He handed the arrow back to her. "Too short for my bow, lad. But I thank you just the same."

He picked up his quarterstaff and longbow. "I'll lead you to Robin's camp, shall I?"

Her heart started to thump, and her throat tightened so fearsomely that she could not speak. She nodded. Let him call her "lad" if he wanted. He was one of Robin Hood's men, he really was. And he was taking her to meet her father.

"This way." He led off along the stream.

Ro followed, watching him and trying to walk the way he walked, with a padding heel-to-toe stride that barely rustled the leaves underfoot. Whenever she tried to move silently through a forest she went slowly, but this man strode along as if he were on his way to London, yet made hardly any sound. He slipped sideward between saplings and did not rattle a twig. He ducked branches without slackening his pace. Ro tried to keep up with him at a walk, but had to give it up and trot after him, crashing her way though the thickets.

"What's your name?" she asked. Maybe talking would slow him down.

But he only gave her a smiling glance. "An outlaw like you," he said, "should know better than to go asking a man in green his name."

"Oh." Ro clenched her teeth. He was teasing her. He did not seem to care whether she could keep up with him or not. She was a ragtag skittering at his tail, that was all. She said nothing more as she toiled along, trying not to make quite as much noise as a charging boar.

He took her across the stream by a zigzag of rocks, not wetting so much as the toes of his boots, while Ro slipped and stumbled behind him and Ty splashed them both. On the other side, the man in green led the way up a hillside so steep that Ro had to clutch trees to keep from sliding back at each step.

At the top he paused, but not for breath. He lifted his head, puckered his lips and gave a cheery whistle, like a robin redbreast at nesting time.

"To let them know all is well," he explained to Ro, who stood panting beside him. "So they don't meet us with drawn bows. Just the same," he added, throwing a wry glance toward Ty, who was trying to run up a chestnut tree after a squirrel, "you'd better keep that pet of yours in hand, sweet little puppy dog that he is."

"Ty!" Rosemary called him to walk beside her as they headed down the other side of the hill.

Her heart pounded so fiercely she could hear it in her ears. Within a few moments she would meet Robin Hood, her father, and what would she say to him? Would she tell him that she was his daughter?

But—no, why should she? She didn't trust him. Why in all her thirteen years had he never come to her or sent for her? What if he just didn't care?

She followed the fair-haired man down into a hollow as round as some giant's supper bowl. Then her eyes widened, for in the center of the hollow stood the mightiest oak she had ever seen, its trunk as big around as her mother's cottage had been. Under the shelter of its massive branches, a score or more of green-clad outlaws had gathered. Some of them were placing a whole deer over a bed of coals to roast, some of them fletching arrows, some sitting at ease. Most of them turned to stare as Ro and her guide walked into camp.

"Robin," somebody called, "what have you there?"

Rosemary felt everything in her stop. Her breath, her heartbeat, her feet. She stood wooden at the edge of the clearing.

"I thought you were going to fetch us a rich merchant, Robin," someone else shouted, "to feast withal."

"Not a skinny beggar and—what is that? A wolf?"

"Which one?" Robin shot back.

Rosemary's heart came to life again, painfully. It was him. Her father. Robin Hood.

And already he had tricked her.

Eight

Business had to wait until after dinner. That was one of Robin's rules. Ro had to sit at the place of honor by the fire. Another rule. Robin led her to the cushion of deerskins the outlaws had piled there, saw her seated, settled himself nearby and said, "Well, now that you know my name, what's yours, lad?"

A broth of emotions barely let her reply. He was so handsome, manly, strong, brave, everything a girl could want in a father. His smile was so droll and sweet. And she was so angry with him for playing a trick on her and making her feel like a fool. The anger gave edge to her tone as she answered, "Ro."

"Roe? That's a deer." He did not say "my dear little lad," but she saw it in his smile.

She clenched her teeth. "Rowan," she told him. She had thought about this. If the girl Ro was named after a goodly herb, then the boy Ro would be named after a goodly tree.

"Well, Rowan, my lad, you look as if you could stand a good meal. Eat your fill."

They loaded her trencher with whole quail and venison and roast suckling pork dipped in honey. They gave her oatcakes and barley bread and dried-apple pudding. They gave her sweet yellow cheese and salt biscuit with spiced cider to drink. The food was so good that she tried to eat, but she could not swallow much. Her throat felt tight.

The outlaws talked and laughed and joked more loudly than harvesters after the wheat is cut, chattering worse than the starlings in the oak boughs overhead. A burly outlaw paused as he passed Rowan's seat, on his way to fetch more food. "Pretty little doggie," he said owlishly to Tykell, who lay at Ro's feet.

"Poor wee lapdog," said another. "What are you doing in the woods, poor wee thing?"

"What is such a wee bitty dog doing with such a great tall outlaw?" called another sarcastically.

Ro set down her bread and stared, for she did not care to be mocked.

"A great tall outlaw," added a green-clad man shorter than the rest, "with fine fancy peacock—"

"Now, Much, don't begrudge him," Robin put in. "The arrows were given to him. By an overdoting aunt, most likely."

Ro's eyes widened at a thought: This was perhaps almost true. The aelfe, her kin, had gifted her with the arrows. But why?

Taking Robin's hint with good cheer, the outlaws laughed and talked of other things. Ro sat back from her trencher and sighed.

"Eat," Robin urged. "Have some more cider."

"Thank you, but I—I've had enough." She could not eat or drink. She felt too small.

"Why, if you've eaten enough, then," said Robin, "it's time for the entertainment." He called to the short outlaw, "Much! Give us a song!"

They all joined in a ditty about hunting the red deer. Compared to the honey-voiced minstrel Ro had heard, they sang like a rookery of jackdaws. But they roared out the song with such glee that, listening, she had to smile.

"A bout!" Robin cried. "Who'll stand me a bout?"

A dozen or more of them sprang up, swinging their quarterstaffs—straight cudgels made of toughest oak, each as long as its owner was tall. Pairing off, the outlaws struck at one another, jabbing and feinting, till the forest echoed with the hard crack of oak against oak. Looking on from her place of honor by the fire, one hand on Tykell's warm, solid back, Ro tried not to wince with the sound of each blow. She watched Robin Hood spar and parry, *crack, crack*— then came the sound of a worse whack, wood against bone, as Robin overpowered his opponent's defense and walloped him on the head. The man fell and lay still.

"One for me," declared Robin cheerfully, standing over the fallen outlaw. "Get up, Will."

On the ground, the man groaned and tried to lift himself, then rolled over and lay still. Ro saw blood darkening his hair. She clenched her teeth and clutched at Tykell's fur.

"Cry mercy, then," said Robin to the outlaw.

"Mercy," he mumbled.

Every instinct in Ro urged her to run to the hurt man and help him, bandage him, comfort and heal him, but her mind told her she had to stay where she was. Badly wanting to tell Robin Hood what she thought of him and his quarterstaff, she pressed her lips together and hung on to Ty.

Reaching down, Robin gave the felled outlaw a hand and hauled him to his feet, then looked around at the others. Taut, sweating, their faces grim, they were sparring hard, oaken staff cracking against oaken staff. "Enough," Robin called, and they stepped back from each other, panting, letting their quarterstaffs sag to the ground. Rowan breathed out.

"Archery," Robin ordered.

A young outlaw ran across the clearing and far into the shadows of the forest. Wondering, Ro watched him cut the bark away from a sapling so that the white wood showed. That was the mark? So far away she could barely see it?

"Little John!" Robin called.

Ro looked at the short outlaw, whose name she had forgotten, but instead, a rugged giant of a man strode forward, carrying the longest, strongest yew bow Rowan had ever seen. Setting its tip against his heel, he strung it with one easy movement of his big hands, then took his stance and shot three arrows at the mark. Instead of aiming above it to allow for the distance, he aimed level at it, and the yard-long goose-fletched arrows sprang from his bow with such force that they carried straight to the target, burying their heads in the wood. Rowan blinked and murmured, "Great toads!" as two out of the three shafts hit the mark.

"Good," Robin remarked to Little John with his merriest smile, "but let me see if I can do better." Easy as thought, he leaned into his bow and sent three arrows winging toward the mark, all three in the air as the first one reached the mark, *thwock.* Then *thwock, thwock,* and Rowan gasped: Robin's arrows clustered on the mark like three bees on a white flower.

No one else seemed surprised. Little John just grinned.

"Much, the miller's son!" Robin called next.

The short outlaw took his turn and put two arrows in the mark. One after the other, each of Robin's men took three shots at the mark, and all of them hit it at least once—until the young outlaw who had set up the target took his turn. He tried hard, taking careful aim, but all three of his arrows flew wide.

"A buffet!" Robin cried as if calling for a treat. Before Ro knew what was happening, Little John stepped forward and walloped the youngster in the chest so hard he fell sprawling. Ro bit back a cry, but the "merry men" roared with laughter. How could they laugh? Yet the young outlaw got up and grinned as if being knocked down were great fun.

"Will Scathelock!" Robin called the next outlaw to shoot.

It was the man Robin had struck down with his quarterstaff. He wore a rag around his bloodied head now. Ro held her breath as he shot, for he was injured, maybe his hurt head would make him shoot badly, and—would Little John hit him, too?

She need not have worried. Will Scathelock put two out of three arrows in the mark.

Ro knew that if she had tried to hit that target, she would have taken a buffet from Little John.

The forest shadows grew longer as more outlaws took their turns. Under towering elms, the white mark stood in deep green shade now. As the arrows whizzed, Tykell watched with lifted head and greatest interest but stayed where he was, by Ro's side.

Robin turned to her. "Rowan, lad, show the men what your dog can do!"

She shook her head. "Tykell is not a clown for your merriment."

Robin blinked. There was a moment of tense silence.

"Do you want me to beat some sense into the lad's head, Robin?" Little John growled.

"Saints, no. I like a bold lad who speaks truth." Robin turned to the others. "Has everyone shot? One more song, then."

They shouted a bawdy ditty about a knight who wore his sword too long, and then with much noise they set to cleaning up after the feast. Ro heard quarrelsome voices and saw two men face off, shoving at each other. Robin brushed past them as if nothing were happening, came and sat by Ro again.

"Now, then," he said, "you want to join my band."

She nodded, although she no longer felt sure about this.

"How came you to be outlawed, lad?"

She bit her lip and looked, not at him, but at hazel bushes growing along one edge of the clearing, at a wren perched on a hazel limb, catching the last ray of sunlight like a spark. She did not want to talk about the burned cottage, about her mother lying there dead.

"Is there a price on your head?" Robin asked.

She looked down at the loamy ground. "No," she mumbled.

"Then you're not an outlaw, are you?"

If she wasn't, she should have been. "I've shot the king's deer." Only royalty were allowed to hunt deer; many a hungry peasant had been outlawed for poaching them.

"Then you're a bold lad. But has the king noticed?"

"No, I suppose not. But—"

"You have no need to stay here, then."

"But—but I have nowhere else to go."

"Surely—"

"Guy of Gisborn says he is going to kill me," Ro interrupted. She had almost forgotten about this until she considered that it might make her an outlaw.

Robin straightened and gave her a startled look. "Guy of Gisborn?"

"You know him?"

"I've heard of him. Does he really wear a horsehide, tail and all?"

"Yes. Well—I didn't notice a tail."

"He wants to kill you?"

"Because I would not give him my bow and arrows. Yes."

"He fancied your peacock arrows, forsooth."

"No. I just had this kind then." Rowan's bow and quiver lay close at hand. She leaned over and pulled out one of her crude wooden-tipped arrows to show Robin. "No one would ever fancy these. But I never asked for peacock arrows," she added.

"You're a fine arrow of a lad." Robin gave her a level, quiet look. "Let me try to do you a favor. Rowan, lad, it's no lark to be an outlaw. It's what you've seen, but it's suffering, too, and being out always in the wet and cold, and it's bloodshed, and not knowing when someone might take a notion to hang you or cut your head off, and it's never being able to go home. If there's somewhere—"

"There's not."

"Surely some lord would take you into his service."

She shook her head, stroking Ty. Even if it had been true before, it was not now. Wherever she went from now on, Ty went with her. And she could not imagine any lord welcoming Ty into his service.

"I see," Robin said, although she had said nothing.

They sat in silence for a few moments. Sundown had turned to twilight, and the forest stood stark against a dimming sky. Something as gray and noiseless as a ghost swooped low over the clearing—an owl beginning its night's hunting. In the oak boughs spreading overhead, Ro heard the sleepy twittering of songbirds nesting for the night. They had homes.

"Well," said Robin after a while, "the rule is this: Any man who wishes to join my band must best me at something. Quarterstaff, maybe, or wrestling, or shooting with the bow." Although no one had ever bested him at marksmanship, the tales said. "Can you wrestle me to the ground?"

"I doubt it," Ro said.

"Drub me with a staff?"

"I might be able to beat you in a game of horseshoes."

"You ought to go home, lad."

"I have no home."

She felt him studying her and looked at him, meeting his gaze. There was no blue spark of fun in his eyes now—they seemed as gray as the twilight, clouded with thought. "Well," he said slowly, "you could stay as a kind of apprentice. There are a thousand tasks you could help with. If—"

A movement at the edge of the clearing caught Ro's eye. One of the outlaws stood there, pissing against a tree.

He stood with his back mostly to her, and his jerkin covered most of that, so it was not the sight that jolted her so much as the thought: If she stayed here, they would take their pants down in front of her. And they would expect her to take *hers* down in front of *them*.

"If you'll promise, as the others do," Robin was saying, "to obey me—"

Not if it meant being walloped by Little John, she wouldn't. She would never promise to obey anyone. "I will not be a servant."

Robin's eyebrows lifted like hawk wings. "We keep no servants. We are all yeomen here."

"Just the same." Ro stood up, feeling her dreams

crashing to shards around her feet. "Thank you for—for everything, Robin. I can see that I was a fool to come here. I'll go now."

"What?" Robin Hood scrambled to his feet, looking almost as astonished as he had when Tykell had snatched his bolt out of the air. "Wait. There's no need—"

Ro picked up her bow and her quiver of arrows. Ty stood wagging by her knee; she touched him for the sake of his warm strength. "Thank you," she said again, looking at her wolf-dog, not quite able to look at Robin. She turned away.

Robin Hood caught her gently by the arm. "There's no need to go off into the dark!" Beyond the campfire light, Ro could see only black nightfall shadows, and from somewhere in the benighted forest a fox yowled. Robin urged her, "Stay, warm yourself by the fire, sleep in a safe bed. In the morning we can talk again."

She shook her head, knowing she had to leave right then; she felt tears stinging her eyes. "Thank you, but no," she whispered, and she pulled away from the touch of his hand. With Ty trotting by her side, she strode away.

"The Lady be with you, then," Robin called after her.

Nine

R o slept under a blackthorn tree, without bed or blanket or campfire, curled up against Ty.

At daylight she sat up and raked the leaves from her hair with her fingers, shivering. All around her, trees loomed silent amid dank gray mist. Ro whacked herself, flailing her arms to try to feel warm and alive, then gave it up, lifted her bow and stood up feeling as empty as her belly.

"Confound Robin," she muttered, "why does he have to make everything so hard?"

It was his fault she had left his camp almost in tears. But she hadn't cried after all, and she couldn't cry now. Her eyes felt burning dry, as if all her tears had turned to stone in her chest. She had not been able to cry since—since that day. The cottage lying in ashes.

Ty looked up at her, furry and blinking.

"Now what?" she asked him. The gray day pressed down on her. "I have nowhere to go."

Unless she told Robin Hood the truth, confound him.

But he was such a fox—could she trust him? She wanted to. She liked his smile. But what was she to do, tell him she was his son? He would not want her if he knew she was a girl. No one wanted girls except as servants.

All around her leaves and twigs drooped, dripping in the fog.

"I suppose I ought to just . . . move on. . . ."

Ty yawned, stood up and stretched himself, bowing like a courtier. Then he shook himself, sat down and scratched. He had fleas. So did Ro, from sleeping in the leaves with him. At home she would have bathed to get rid of them.

It was no use thinking of home. She had no home. No mother.

No father.

"So," she murmured to Ty and the gray day, "which way?" It was no longer a matter of waiting for the mist to clear, then heading a bit south of the rising sun, toward Sherwood Forest.

"Toads take it!"

Rosemary sat down on the ground again. She sat there so long that the morning mist made wraiths of itself and swirled away, the early sun slanted watery through the leaves. By Ro's side, Ty lay waiting.

She whispered, "I can't just leave."

She looked up and took a deep breath, her decision made. She had to see Robin Hood again. Maybe it was no use, but she could not give up—not yet. She had come too far to just go away. And she wanted to know. The truth: What kind of father was Robin Hood? Why had he never acknowledged her?

She got up and started gathering wild onions and mushrooms for a breakfast of sorts. "Tykell," she told the wolf-dog, "we'll watch, that's what we'll do. We'll find out what he's really like. We'll see whether the ballads speak truth."

The ballads said nothing of this, but—maybe she would even be able to find out whether he had other children. Other girls. And how he treated them.

Then—then she was not sure what.

But one thing at a time. "We'll start by watching the road," Ro told Tykell, for the Nottingham Way ran through Sherwood Forest. "If we see a rich traveler, we'll follow. We'll see whether Robin Hood waylays him. And whether he's as courteous about it as folk say."

Where the road forded the stream, Ro found good cover in a tangle of grape that gave her a vantage. Sitting with her back against a stump, she waited, watching the road—not a dusty thoroughfare here, but a grassy path snaking through the forest, green and shady, pleasant for the traveler if it were not for the danger of being robbed.

Ro saw a ragged tinker go by, his donkey rattling with kettles and pots and pans, and she wondered what he would do if she went down and pointed an arrow at him and told him to give her one. The sun glared down at noon, and she saw a straw-hatted old pilgrim man hobble along, leaning on his staff. Ty got bored and wandered off. Ro sat. Ants crawled on her. The sun moved on, and she saw some lord's messenger boy on his shaggy pony. She dozed in the afternoon warmth, made herself wake up, saw a fat, floury miller riding a mule. She saw two women leading an ox. Nothing more. The sun slid toward the west. Rosemary's belly knotted with hunger. Time to go hunt for dinner—

Rosemary sat bolt upright, her eyes widening. From the south, a shining cavalcade jangled down to the ford.

At first Ro could barely sort it out, red pennons and armor ringing like bells and the water leaping silver from under steely hooves as the foremost horses splashed into the ford. Then she began to see how the men-at-arms rode two by two, six couples of them in basin helms and quilted tunics, and how three knights in chain mail flanked them, swallowtail flags fluttering from the upraised tips of their lances. A white rose on a red ground—Ro did not recognize the insignia and she did not care. Surely this small army guarded a rich treasure. Surely these were travelers whom Robin would rob. The wagon was coming into view—

By the Lady.

Pulled by four matched dapple-gray horses, the wagon rippled with garlands of cloth-of-gold and red pennons and white satin rosettes, every inch of it bedecked except the rims of the wheels. At the four corners of the wagon stood four white lances, and between the lance tips hung a sunshade of red cloth with white ribbons fluttering down from the edges.

And under this red cloth roof, on cushions covered with gold damask, rode—a girl. A girl in a white jeweled gown.

Ro gasped and blinked. For a moment she felt as if it could have been her sitting there. The princess—that girl had to be a princess—looked no bigger or older than Ro was, her pale face riding very small under her white linen headdress studded with pearls and bound with gold. The heart-shaped caul hid her hair entirely, so that Ro could not tell what color it was. *Probably golden tresses perfectly curled,* Ro thought. Two grim-looking women in black rode with the princess, but Ro barely noticed them—she was thinking that this girl did not sleep on roots and stones, this girl's belly had never been knotted with hunger. The cavalcade slowed almost to a halt while the wagon eased through the ford to keep from splashing the princess, so Ro had plenty of time to stare, hot with envy. Look at that gown, white satin with a white silk overgown with gold-bordered sleeves that flowed to the ground. Ro hoped that Robin Hood would rob every single jewel—

But the ballads said that Robin Hood would not trouble any company with a woman in it.

Why so many guards, then? Behind the wagon rode six pair of men-at-arms again, and more knights.

Rosemary watched them pass, then got up, stiff from sitting so long, and followed.

Keeping to the woods above the road, as silently as she could, she made her way, trotting sometimes to stay abreast of the cavalcade. She worried briefly about Ty, then made herself stop worrying. She had to learn to trust him. He had found her before, and he would find her again. Anyway, the riders and their precious princess could not go too much farther. Already the shadows grew long. Soon night would halt them.

Look. They were stopping already.

They had come to Fountain Dale, a place where the road widened into a meadow and a spring ran down into a stone basin. Watching from a distance, Ro saw a muddle of men and horses and heard shouting. Was Robin attacking at last? No. It was just that they were trying to get water and make camp.

The thought of camp and food made her hungry stomach ache harder. This had been a wasted day, and she had not shot herself anything to eat, and now she felt almost too starved to stand and hunt. Thrushes whistled and scolded in a clump of holly nearby, getting settled for the night. Ro went and found a nest within her reach, scratching her arms and hands on the prickly leaves as she parted the branches. The parent birds flapped around her head and shrieked at her as she took four small speckled eggs, cracked them one by one into her mouth and gulped them down. It was not much food, but enough to quiet her belly and keep her going until she could find her own source of water and a place to sleep.

Where was Ty? Maybe he would bring her a mangled rabbit to eat. Likely that silk-gowned princess was eating marzipan and crumpets right now. Rosemary rolled her eyes at the thought, then put it behind her, turning her back on it, walking away.

But she stopped as a fierce, frightened yell sounded from one of the men making camp in Fountain Dale. "Where is she?"

A hubbub of shouting arose.

"Is she over there?"

"Who was supposed to be watching her?"

"Did anybody see which way—"

"She's not anywhere! She's gone!"

One angry voice rose above the rest. "Fan out, men! Find her, or we're all gallows meat!"

There wasn't time for Rosemary to reason it out. All she could think was that they were after her, and every inch of her hummed like a bowstring with alarm. She heard branches rattle behind her, grabbed for an arrow as she swung around—

The white-gowned princess came running through the holly, her face as taut as a flayed hide, her eyes like those of a hunted deer.

Ten

Scratched bloody, panting, and stumbling in her too-long skirt, the white-gowned girl lunged through the thicket toward Ro yet seemed not to see her.

With her strung bow in one hand and her arrow in the other, Ro stood still, not knowing what to do. She had envied this girl? The terror in those wide eyes made her forget her envy. She had to help—

But how? Save the princess from—from what?

The forest rang with shouts and the sounds of trampling hooves, branches rattling and snapping. An armed knight came clattering up the hill toward Ro.

Ro stepped back behind the trunk of an oak. She wore brown; he might not have seen her. But the princess in her linen headdress and glossy silken gown stood out like a white fluttering butterfly in the darkening woods. She stumbled and fell on the loamy slope, scrambled up and ran a few paces and stumbled again. She lost one white slipper, then the other, and ran on, barefoot. But she could not run nearly fast enough. The knight rode up to her, looming over her on his tall bay charger.

Just the way he looked down on her made Ro's fist tighten on her bow. Where was Robin Hood?

"I have her," called the knight to Sherwood Forest, sounding cold and bored. "Come, my lady." His voice crawled with scornful courtesy. "Let me escort you back to—"

She darted away from him. He sent his horse after her and past her, blocked her way, and dismounted.

"Come, now, my lady." He seized her by the arm and pulled her toward the horse.

She did not make a sound. Ro had not yet heard a sound from her except her panting breath. But her body screamed, twisting. She kicked, and at the same time she writhed so vehemently that she broke away. She ran. But she had not taken three steps before the knight caught her by the shoulder, spun her around and struck her across the face with his gauntleted hand so hard that she fell.

"Stop it!" Rosemary yelled. She ran toward them,

then thought better of it, took an archer's stance and drew her bow, her arrow leveled at him.

He swung around as if a puppy were pestering him and he needed to kick it. "What is this?" Shoulders hunched, fists curled, he peered at her from under his helm. "Woods colt," he said, "do you think your dart can hurt me? You need a thrashing." He started toward her, his mail jangling. Behind him, the runaway lady was struggling to her feet. *Maybe if I can busy him a moment . . .* Ro thought. Hoping the girl still had strength to run away, she loosed her arrow at the knight. As she had expected, it merely blunted itself against his mailed chest and fell to the ground. He roared out a curse and shook his fist at her, hastening his heavy, armored stride. Lips pressed together, Ro backed off a few feet as she snatched at her quiver for another—

A stick snapped, and the knight glanced over his shoulder. "You!" he roared at the white-clad girl. He ran back to her as she tottered away from him, seized her and struck her again, holding her so that she would not fall. Her head swung back and her eyes closed. He hauled her toward the horse.

"Don't!" bawled a male voice. "You big bully!"

Ro blinked. In the dusk she did not see where he came from, but there facing the knight stood the giant baby-faced minstrel, red curly-tipped shoes and quail-feathered hat and all. "You're not nice!" he accused.

"Out of my way, churl." The knight tried to shove him aside.

The shove had no effect. The minstrel did not move. "Only a *coward* hits a lady," he complained.

"Out of my way, you oversized lout!" The knight struck the giant boy's chest with his steel-armored fist.

"Ow! That hurt!" wailed the boy. Like an enraged toddler he swatted at the knight's helmeted face. But his clumsy blow missed entirely. Instead, he hit the horse on the head.

The horse squealed and fell down.

For a moment no one moved or spoke. Ro stood with her mouth open and her bow and arrow sagging. The knight looked at the horse lying on the ground. He looked down at the boy's feet, which were after all not quite as large as the downed horse's head, maybe more the size of a pony's. Then he looked up at the boy's face, a foot above his own. Without a word, he let go of the girl and reached for his sword.

"Meanie," the minstrel complained, swatting again, his open hand clanging against the knight's helm.

Ro darted past the pair of them toward the girl, who had somehow stayed on her feet, tottering. "Come on." Ro grabbed her around the shoulders and hustled her away, into the shadows of Sherwood. Behind her she heard the thud of a blow—but whose? All around sounded the yells and crashings of the other men still searching.

They had not run nearly far enough before the girl stumbled on her skirt and fell to her knees. And they would not be able to go far, Ro knew, with the lady gleaming like a beacon in the night. Ro snatched the linen headdress off her head and hurled it away. The girl's hair tumbled down, not golden after all, but long and brown. As the girl struggled up, Ro caught at her jeweled, silken gown and ripped it open, pulling it off her and flinging it after the headdress. Now the girl stumbled a few steps barelegged, wearing nothing but a chemise—but the chemise lustered like moonlight. "Aren't you wearing anything that isn't *white*?" Ro wailed.

The lady looked at her but did not answer. Red marks flamed on her white face, already her left eye was blackening and swelling shut, and she seemed not to understand anything that was happening.

"Here," said a husky voice.

Ro jumped, but did not reach for her bow. It was

the minstrel, towering over both of them, pulling a dark cloak from one of his packs. "Wrap that around her."

"You're all right!" Ro blurted. She had not let herself think about it much, but she had expected the knight had lopped him to pieces by now.

"No, I'm *not*. I hurt my *hand*," the large boy whined as he wrapped the cloak around the girl himself.

"Shhh!" Ro hushed him as clatterings and crashings drew nearer.

"Over here!" a man brayed.

"Her gown—still warm."

The minstrel picked up the swaddled princess, cradled her in his arms and strode off into the darkness.

"She can't have gone far."

"Hurry! Bring torches!"

Trotting after the minstrel, Ro heard the shouts almost in her ears to both sides and much too near behind her. Fear was a gauntleted hand choking her throat. What would they do to her if they caught her? The minstrel strode uphill into rough terrain, and Ro stayed close behind him—better to be captured with others than alone—but she flinched every time he rattled branches or stumbled against a rock, making a noise. The big lummox blundered right into a patch of bracken, rustling like a hundred deer. "Shhhh!" Ro hissed, and they all stood still, listening for pursuit. But the uproar behind them seemed to be fading off in the wrong direction. A few torches showed near Fountain Dale, far down the hillside.

"They can't hear us," the minstrel said, keeping his voice low. "They're making more noise than we are." He moved off again.

"Do you know where you're going?" Ro asked.

"No, I don't." He sounded peevish, as if this were all her fault. "And I'm *hungry,* and my *hand* hurts, and I—"

"My head hurts worse than your hand," said an unexpected voice.

The minstrel stood still and peered down at the bundle in his arms. "My dear lady, you don't have to strum a harp with your head," he said.

"I'm not your dear lady. Put me down, please. I can walk."

He set the girl upon her feet but kept a hand on her arm to support her. She pulled away from him and walked on, wavering.

"If you're not a dear lady," Ro asked, walking beside her, "then what are you?"

"Ettarde."

"That's a lady name if I ever heard one. Are you a princess?"

"No. Not anymore." The girl sounded quiet and grim. She had a soft, vibrant voice that reminded Ro of the way wood thrushes talk in their nests at night. Walking, she passed from shadow into moonlight, and Ro lost a breath at the sight of her face, pale on one side, bruised black on the other, with hot red streaks to mark the impact of the knight's hand.

"You need cold water," Ro said, breath returning with a rush of urgency. Water, healing herbs, comfrey—Ro felt her hands lift toward the hurt girl, wanting to take care of her.

"So do *I*," complained the large minstrel from just behind them.

Water. Ro knew it was up to her to help the other two. She was the only one not injured, and she carried herbs and bandaging in her pouch—but where could she find water in the dark, in this rocky upland?

"*And* I need something to eat," the minstrel grumbled on, "but where—"

Ro paid no attention, for something odd was happening inside her, like a tug at the stem of her heart.

She stopped so suddenly that the big lout bumped into her from behind.

"What the—"

"Shhh." Something was calling to her like a silent song, and it took Ro about seven heartbeats to understand, and when she did comprehend, the knowledge pooled in her like tears.

Use the gifts your mother gave you, daughter of Celandine.

It was water, secret water somewhere amid rocks and moss, ferns and ivy, perhaps hidden between tall Sherwood oaks wearing crowns of mistletoe, perhaps beneath a twisted blackthorn. Ro felt something of holy, healing trees and—hidden, hidden sweetwater close at hand, pulling at her heart. Pure drinking water, hollow-hill water from the heart of the earth, like Celandine's spring. Amid all the commotion of the night echoing in her heart, Ro could sense its presence, although faintly. It seemed that she had inherited some small portion of her mother's power after all.

"This way," she said, leading off.

"Where are we going?"

"You'll see."

Following, the minstrel let out a hefty sigh and

directed his next comment to the princess. "Why were they beating you, my lady?"

"Ettarde."

"Um, Ettarde. Why were you running away?"

Instead of answering, Ettarde asked, "What is your name?"

"Um, Lionel, my—" He stopped himself from calling her "my lady."

She asked, "And you, archer?"

Leading them over a stony shoulder of the hillside into an even rockier ravine, it took Ro a moment to realize that Ettarde was speaking to her. "Oh! I'm Ro—" She almost said Rosemary. "Rowan."

"Lionel. Rowan." It would seem that Ettarde was accustomed to formalities. Even walking barefoot through a wilderness in her chemise with a borrowed cloak wrapped messily around her, she sounded courtly. "I thank you both greatly for your help."

"Save your breath for walking," Ro said, more gruffly than she intended. She thought she heard the call of secret water in her heart, but how could she be sure? Maybe she was crazy. The rocks had given way to boulders and the boulders to soaring, mossy crags. They were stumbling into the roughest wilderness she had yet seen in Sherwood Forest. In the dark. With a small army after them.

Eleven

"T his way," Ro said, keeping her voice down so that the enemy would not hear her. The call of springwater tugged stronger in her, giving her an odd sureness, almost a sense of protection, as if her mother's green power mantled her. *This way to safety,* the spirit of water seemed to whisper to her. *This way, and no men on horseback will come near you.* She led the way up a slope so steep that she had to hang on to the saplings growing out of the cracks in the rock.

"Are you *insane?*" Lionel bleated.

"Shush!" Ro snapped at him, because maybe she was. Rocks rattled overhead—some wild animal lurked there. Ro could hear it panting in the night. She fell back a couple of paces and grabbed for her bow, then changed her mind and grabbed for Ettarde instead, placing a hand over the girl's mouth just as she started to scream. Green moonlit eyes, the gleam of white teeth—with great panting happiness, Tykell bounded down from a crag to meet them.

"Hush," Ro told Ettarde. "He will not hurt you."

"Wolf!" she gasped.

"He's not. He's my dog." Ro let go of Ettarde and scolded Tykell. "Where in the name of mercy have you *been* all day?"

Farther down the slope, Lionel reported, "Now I stubbed my *toe.*"

"Oh, for—" Ro decided to save her breath for the climb. "It's not much farther." She hoped it was not much farther. The hankering that had taken hold of her heart had sharpened to a knifepoint of yearning. "Come on." She led the way sharply upward, between the rocks and trees, with Tykell scrabbling along beside her.

"You *are* insane," Lionel said morosely.

Ro did not answer.

Halfway up the craggy hillside she found it.

The rocks formed a cup screened by trees—Ro could see no more than that in the darkness, but she could hear the spring now. Standing in the hollow of rock as if in the palm of some earth-giant's hand, she could almost smell the sweetwater. Its presence tugged at her like homesickness.

She could not see it, but it was there. Hidden. In the rocks.

Tykell snuffed deeply at a crack low on the side of one craggy wall.

"By your leave," Ro whispered to the spirit of water as she knelt. "Thank you, Lady of this place." She felt the stone, then lifted at it as the other two came panting up beside her. The rock budged under her fingers, but just barely.

"Lionel. Bring your muscles here."

"My hand is *hurt*," Lionel objected. "I hurt it on that knight." His voice shivered. "What if I—what if I hurt *him*?"

Ro looked up at him in the darkness, for the first time understanding what he had risked and how frightened he was. If he had maimed the knight or killed him, saving Ettarde, then there would be a blood-price on his head.

"I'm sorry," she told him. She could not think what else to say.

Ettarde knelt beside Ro at the rock and tugged at it. Both pulling together, they moved it slightly.

"We need a stick to pry it up," Ettarde said.

"Oh, for pity's sake." Lionel took hold of the stone with his left hand and heaved it over. It thudded aside, and in the hollow where it had been ran a moonlit shimmer of pure water.

"Good. We're home." Ro felt a prickle of uncanny joy as she said the words, for they were true. This was now her home, she who had none. No one else knew of this spring. It was hers.

Tykell gave a single low woof. Ro had slept for only two hours, but she awoke at once, reaching for her bow. Day was just breaking. Silvergold light filtered through the feathery leaves of the trees ringing Ro's sanctuary, and Sherwood Forest stood as hushed as the light. Even the birds were not stirring yet. Ro heard no sound. But Ty stood with front feet atop the rocks and his ears pricked, staring uphill as if someone were coming.

Ty wagged his tail.

Ro stood and silently climbed a few steps up the rocks above the spring. Just as she stopped to look around, there was a breath in the air and the stirring of a single leaf. In the next breath, Robin Hood stood beside her.

"Rowan, lad." Robin looked around and smiled. "Of course. In a rowan grove."

Ro looked at the slender trees haloed in the dawn light, aspiring like dancers all around her, and she felt a prickling of the same uncanny joy as she had sensed when she found the spring: This was *her* place. Her home, although she had never been there before.

For a moment she could not speak. Then she said, "I didn't know, in the dark." She kept her voice down, for Etty and Lionel were still sleeping.

Looking down over the lip of the rocky hollow at them, Robin lost his smile. Ettarde lay wrapped in Lionel's mantle, her face too pale except for her bruised cheek and eye, swollen and dark. Robin said softly, "So that's the princess."

"Not anymore." Ro gave him a sharp look. "How do you know?" And if he did know so much, where was he when she needed him? She had just spent most of the night nursing Etty with cold compresses and comfrey poultices—and Lionel, too, just so that he would not whimper, although she could see nothing wrong with his hand at all. But she had used up all her wound worts on the pair of them, in between the hours she had spent preparing wake-robin root, which was all they had to eat. The miserable weed had to be rinsed and soaked and rinsed and mashed and rinsed again before the bite was rinsed out of it, and maybe Ro had left some in. She sounded fit to bite as she demanded, "And if you know so much, where were you?" Where was Robin Hood, the great hero, while she was stuck taking care of everyone?

He might have felt the same way, because he lowered his head and gave her a wry look from under his brows. "We were playing catch-the-arrow with Ty."

She stood speechless.

"He fetched hundreds for us," Robin said. "The men had never seen anything like it. But now all our arrows have fang marks in them."

Ro found her voice. "And meanwhile—"

"Then, on toward dusk we heard a great to-do and hullabaloo," Robin went on as if she had not spoken, "and we went to see what was happening. Will Scathelock found this." He reached deep into his quiver and handed her a short arrow, peacock-fletched. An elf-bolt.

The one that had fallen to the ground when she shot at the knight.

She accepted it from him, feeling all her ire seep away like the springwater running into the rocky ground. "Thank you," she said softly. "It could have gone badly with me if they had found it instead of you." Her back chilled just from thinking of how badly it could have gone—and she had forgotten all about the arrow until that moment.

"Did you leave any more?"

She thought back, going over Ettarde's flight in her mind, then shook her head. "I don't think so. But—maybe you know. Lionel is worried. He hit a horse by mistake and knocked it down. And then he hit—"

"Lionel?"

Ro pointed her chin toward the massive form of the sleeping minstrel. Wrapped in his blanket, sleeping on a mossy ledge of stone near the spring, he took up half the hollow.

"Him!"

"You know him?"

"He's begged supper from me a time or two. He's a harmless ninny. Is *Lionel* truly his name? It should be Lamb-el."

"True," Ro said.

"If a savage mouse were to cross his path, he might faint. He *what?*" Robin seemed to have just heard what Ro had said. "He knocked down a *horse?*"

"And a knight. He is frightened that he might have killed the knight."

Robin shook his head. "No, I have heard nothing.

But I will try to find out." With limber ease, Robin folded and settled himself cross-legged on the stone. "Sit down and tell me the story from the start, Rowan, lad."

Ro did. She told him all about it, except that she let him think Tykell had found the spring. The memory of how this place had guided her to itself made her spine tingle. It seemed that she was more truly Celandine's daughter than she knew, but she could not speak of it yet. Maybe not ever. If she acknowledged such power, she might suffer her mother's fate. She might be killed for being a witch.

But other than that, she told Robin everything. It felt good to talk to him. Almost as if he were her father.

She found herself telling him Ettarde's story as Ettarde had told it to her and Lionel the night before. It was not an unusual story. Ettarde, age thirteen, was to be given in marriage to a powerful lord with whom her father, a petty king, sought alliance. When Ettarde would not agree to the marriage, she was shut in her tower room and starved. When that did not work, she was sent to the lord under guard. What was unusual about the story was that Ettarde had gotten away.

So far.

"But is she better off?" Robin wondered aloud, his gaze on the sleeping girl.

"Better off than with a hateful old man for a husband? Of course she's better off."

"But what is to become of her?"

"What becomes of anyone on the run? She is an outlaw. You offered to take *me* in . . ." Trying not to let him feel the weight of her stare, Ro watched him.

"Yes," he said, "but a girl?" He shook his handsome golden head, his eyes worried. "What would a girl do in the greenwood?"

Ro looked away from him. It was as she had thought. He did not want her. He would not even want to talk with her if he knew she was a girl.

Twelve

All that day, Sherwood Forest echoed with the crashings and thrashings and shouts of knights and men-at-arms. "They will be searching high and low for her, you know," Robin had said, and he was right. Ro and Lionel and Ettarde stayed where they were and kept their heads down. They were as well hidden in the rowan hollow as anywhere in Sherwood, Robin said, for no one knew there was a spring there—even he had not known. He had found the place only by tracking Tykell.

Tykell stayed, too, and helped the three fugitives eat the food Robin had brought, cold meat and brown bread and cheese. "Somewhat better than wake-robin root," Ettarde remarked, sopping the bread in spring-water before putting it in her sore mouth. She wore Lionel's spare tunic, which covered her to below her knees. With a twinge of her former envy, Ro saw that Etty had bosoms, just large enough to show. Etty probably had monthly courses, too, toads take it. And Etty had the dignity of a true princess. Despite everything, bruised face and bare feet and the odd sort of frock she wore, Etty seemed regally content, like a cottage cat.

"Shhh!" If Ettarde was a cottage cat, Ro was a nervous barn cat, jumping at every sound.

"If you'll look out yonder," grumped Lionel, who had to lie on the stones to stay out of sight, "you'll see a pair of green legs. Or legs in Lincoln green hose, anyway. And in this forest, Lincoln green means—"

"I know." Ro had seen Robin's men guarding them. "Your face is looking better," she said softly to Etty as a kind of apology for having shushed her.

Etty said, "I hope it scars." She kept her voice down, but sounded as if she meant it.

"You do? Why?"

Ettarde answered in a roundabout way. "I have had tutors," she said. "I know how to read and write. I know Latin and French. I understand theology and natural science. But do you know what my father said to Lord Basil's emissaries when he bargained me away?" Her low voice grew yet more intense. "He said that I was a virgin with not a pockmark on my face. It is for the skin of my face that I am to be bought and sold."

Ro did not know what to say. She blurted, "I can't read." Most people couldn't.

Lionel said nothing.

"It's not fair," Ettarde said. "Even if my father doesn't find me, where can I go? How will I live? They won't let me be a scribe or a teacher."

Ro knew just how she felt. "Does your mother have family?"

"No one I can trust not to give me back to my father. I don't know what to do."

"Shhh!" Lionel hissed, even though he was the one who grumbled at Ro's shushings. "Someone's coming."

Someone was already there: Robin Hood. Lionel had not heard him until he was a step away—Robin moved like a spirit through the woods. Lightly, with barely a sound from his soft leather boots, he vaulted down to sit in the rocky hollow among them, his eyes sparkling like blue stars.

"Well," he whispered, "you three have certainly stirred things up after a long, boring winter."

"Oh, lovely," grumped Lionel.

"It's no longer just your entourage that is searching for you, my lady." With his head Robin sketched a kind of bow toward Ettarde. "Now the Sheriff of Nottingham has joined in. He and all his men are out scouring the forest." Robin said this as if it were a great treat for him and all *his* men. Eagerly he turned to Ro. "And guess what other vulture has arrived to circle with the rest of them, Rowan? You'll never guess."

She shook her head. This seemed to be all fun to him, but she did not feel like playing guessing games.

"Guy of Gisborn!"

Rowan felt the world go cold. She could not speak.

"Little John saw him riding into Nottingham," Robin went on, "black horsehide and all. By my troth." Robin sat up straight. "I want to see this apparition for myself." He stared away toward the south, his blue eyes glinting even more brightly than before. "By my poor old body, why am I sitting here in the woods? I know what I am going to do."

Before he even said it, Ro felt foreboding clutch her heart. "Robin, no."

"Oh, yes. It's time for some fun at the good sheriff's expense." He stood to leave.

"Robin," Ro whispered.

"Eh, lad?" He turned back to her, gifting her with his warm, droll smile.

She didn't know what to say to him. She knew

only that she was afraid. Did that make her a coward? She hated feeling so afraid.

"I'm not a lad," she said.

"So you've told me." Robin's smile widened.

"Robin, please don't go to Nottingham."

"Why?"

"The sheriff . . ."

"Him? He's a mother-born idiot." Robin's smile became a grin. "He won't lay a finger on me."

Why was she terrified for him when he had gotten away with such sorties often before? Whatever prank he was planning, she had no sensible reason to beg him not to do it. She had no power over him, either, to make him stay. She could only say, "Please. Be careful."

Late in the day, Ro felt it happening like a change in the weather, like a storm moving into the forest even though the sun still shone. The rowans surrounding her hollow became profoundly still, with not even a single feather-shaped leaf rustling, and she heard grief in their stillness. The motionless air felt heavy and cold, like stone, around her shoulders. Trying to get away from it, not saying anything to the others, she got up and knelt by the spring to drink—

but the water tasted like tears to her. Tears of Sherwood Forest. Tears of earth itself. She began to tremble.

The others did not seem to notice anything—Ettarde lay near the spring listening as Lionel lounged in the hollow, strumming very softly on his harp as if he had forgotten that his hand was supposed to be hurt. Ro told him, "Shhh."

"They won't hear me." It had been hours since there had been any clamor of searchers nearby.

"It's not that. Something has happened."

Lionel laid his harp aside. Ettarde sat up straight and lifted her elegant head like a fallow doe tasting the wind. She turned toward the south, toward Nottingham. Facing that way also, Ro heard murmurs and whispers, then the clatter of pebbles and rustling of rowan leaves as a green-clad outlaw ran up through the rocks, making no effort to be quiet.

"We must leave you," he told the three of them over the lip of the hollow, his tone as flat as the faces of the stones.

"Why?" Ro asked. "What has—"

He was already turning away. She leapt up on the rocks and seized him by the arm.

"Tell me!" she demanded. "Is it Robin?"

"Yes."

"They—please, no. They haven't killed him, have they?"

"Captured," said the man, as stony as before. "They will be wanting to hang him. In the morning."

"But how . . ."

Maybe he felt her hand quivering on his arm, or he saw something in her face. He sighed and turned back toward her. "Robin thought he would have himself a jest," he said in his flat country way. "He put on the clothes of an old soldier and went into Nottingham. He'd done it before. Often." The fellow's voice betrayed some emotion now, if not his face; the words rubbed in his throat. "We don't understand what happened, but—this time—"

"This time the sheriff knew him."

"Yes." The man swallowed and went on. "The sheriff was just coming out of the town hall with that newcomer, Gisborn, and there stood Robin. Sheriff yelled like he saw a ghost, they say. Screamed for the guard. Robin tried to run, but—" The outlaw swallowed again. "He didn't stand a chance."

"Will you—will you and the others—"

"We'll be there when they bring him out to hang him." Some breath of extra quietness in the outlaw's tone told Ro that he was afraid, that he foresaw how much bloodshed there would be, that he thought they might not be able to save Robin that way. He turned away. "I must go now."

She watched after him. When he was gone amid the feathery rowan leaves, she turned to see the others close behind her, leaning over the lip of the hollow, listening.

Somehow within the last five minutes the sun had dimmed and clouds had gathered. Ro was not even surprised when it started to rain, chill gray April rain.

"We have to save Robin," she said to Ettarde and Lionel. She had not known she was going to say the words until they were out of her mouth.

They just looked at her.

"We have to rescue him." Her body felt fevered with worry, but her mind had become a pool of stillness, a cool silver well in which reflections seemed to float, images of what needed to be done. "They'll be expecting an attempt in the morning, so we have to go to Nottingham and get him out now, tonight, while they're celebrating. Lionel." She gazed at the harper. "You go find the sheriff and his men where they are feasting and bind them with the spell of your harp. Ettarde——"

"Whoa! My dear fellow, wait!" Lionel loomed toward her as if he were having trouble following. "You want me to do *what*?"

Why was he being so stupid? "Go to Nottingham," Ro said, making her words quite simple and clear. "Sing and play for the sheriff and his men. Take them into your power. Make them forget everything else. Meanwhile, Ettarde—"

Lionel interrupted again, rearing up like a frightened squirrel. "I can't do that!"

"Of course you can." Ro peered at him; what was the matter with him? "I've heard you sing. You can—"

"I can't sing to *people*! So many of them!"

"You have to." Ro considered the matter settled. She turned to Ettarde. "Etty, while Lionel sings, you and I will get Robin out."

Ettarde, who had remained silent all this time, asked simply, "How?"

"Somehow. I won't know until I see where they're keeping him." Ro broke out of her stance atop the rocks and got moving. "We'll have to disguise you. Tie up your hair, or cut it off—"

"Rowan, stop a minute. Sit down."

The other girl's voice was so gentle yet commanding that Ro actually obeyed. Or partly obeyed. She did not sit down, but she halted where she was and faced Ettarde.

"What happened to keeping me safe?" Ettarde asked. Even with rain running down her bruised face, she spoke as pleasantly as if she were sipping tea. "If I go to Nottingham, I will be showing myself to the people who are hunting me. Why should I do such a crazy thing?"

"And what about me?" Lionel put in, his tone much more plaintive than Ettarde's. "What if I killed that knight? They'll seize me and hang me, too!"

Ro said, "Most likely that knight got up and didn't tell anyone what had happened. Too proud. Ashamed to have been struck down by a boy."

"Yes, but if he's all right, he'll be there with the others. And you want me to *sing to him*?"

Ettarde came to the point—a point like a lance tip. She said, "Why are you asking us to do this insane thing?"

"Asking?" Lionel grumbled. "He's *telling* us."

Ro took a long breath and let it out slowly, realizing that what he said was true. She was trying to tell these two to do something that might cost them their lives.

Ettarde nodded. "Why?" she asked again.

Truth. Ro knew that she owed them the truth. She swallowed hard, swallowing her pride. "Robin Hood," she said, her voice wavering.

"He's a hero," Lionel said. "So? I'm *not*."

"He has his men to help him," Ettarde said.

Ro said, "He's my father."

There was utter silence except for the patter of the rain falling on the rocks, rustling down through the rowan leaves, making rings in the pool of the spring. Etty and Lionel stared at her.

"He doesn't know," Ro added. "I mean, he doesn't know it's me." She couldn't explain anymore. Her voice felt thick. She got herself moving, picking up her bow, gathering her pouch and her quiver of arrows, slinging the things on. "I have to go," she said, not looking at either of them. "I have to try to save him. But I—I can't tell you to come with me. I'll go alone if I have to."

"For pity's sake, Rowan," Lionel complained, "how will you *get* to Nottingham?"

Ro stood looking at him with a hollow feeling in her chest. She hadn't thought of that. Already the sun was going down, and it was no short distance to the town.

"Mercy. My dear fellow, you must learn to *plan* these things." But Lionel stood up and lifted his harp. "Come on. I know what we can do."

Ro did not dare to speak. " 'We'?" echoed Ettarde, a slow smile on her bruised face.

"Of course, 'we.' Aren't you coming?"

"Certainly I am coming. You think I'm going to sit here in the rain? As far as I'm concerned," Ettarde added as she reached for a knife and started hacking off her long, lovely seal-brown hair, "the worst thing about being an outlaw is rain."

Thirteen

They stole horses.

"If we're going to be outlaws," Lionel grumbled, picking his way down the rocky hill, "we might as well *be* outlaws, forsooth. There are perfectly good horses standing idle at Fountain Dale while the men-at-arms search on foot. And speaking of feet, there are Etty's feet to be considered."

Playing the part of a beggar boy, with bare legs and shaggy hair and her face dirtied to hide her bruises, Ettarde only smiled. Ro wondered how much Etty hurt, feet and face and also her chest, where Ro had wrapped tight binding around her bosoms to disguise them.

"I've never ridden a horse," said Ro, trying not to sound like Lionel.

"It's easy," Etty told her.

It wasn't. But stealing the horses was. Unexpectedly easy. Ro hadn't counted on help from Tykell.

It didn't look good for horse-stealing at first. There were guards stationed near the tether line. Bored guards playing chuckfarthing, but still, guards.

"You distract the guards, Lionel," Etty whispered as the three of them crouched in the bushes that crowded the edge of Fountain Dale. "Rowan and I will sneak around and untie three horses—"

"Saddles?" Ro hinted. "Bridles? Something to hang on to?"

Etty just looked at her. Lionel shook his massive head and muttered, "It'll never work."

Ro was about to agree when she happened to notice the glint in Tykell's eyes as he stood beside her. Tykell was staring at the horses with greatest interest. His tail curved up, waving. Ro remembered how he had chased the deer.

"Will it help if Tykell distracts the guards?" she asked. She did not have to worry about Ty's being hurt. If the guards shot at him, he would just leap aside and catch the arrows.

Etty looked at Ty and smiled. Lionel looked at Ty and frowned. "He's going to frighten the *horses*."

"But what else can we do? Try it," Etty said.

Ro told the wolf-dog, "Sic 'em, Ty!"

Tykell gave a woof like a thunderclap and leapt out of the bushes, charging across the clearing toward the horses, barking so hard that he roared.

The result was so quick and thorough that for a moment Ro could only gawk as the horses shrilled and reared and broke their tethers and galloped in several directions. They formed herds by color, as horses will, with the gray horses taking off mostly northward, the bays mostly to the south. The guards jumped up, shouting, and ran after the more valuable dapple grays. Tykell loped after the grays also, yelping happily. Etty, Ro and Lionel looked at one another, then got up and ran in the opposite direction.

They caught three horses a small distance from Fountain Dale. Three dark bays, good for riding at night without being seen. Then, with the guards gone, they dared to go back for saddles and bridles. Etty and Lionel knew how to put them on, but to Ro, the harnesses were all a cat's cradle of leather. After that—the only good thing about the ride to Nottingham, in Ro's opinion, was that it went very quickly, toads take it. She did not actually throw up, although she felt like she might, and she only fell off twice. For the most part she hung on to the mane with both hands, ignoring the reins, and Lionel and Etty rode ahead of her, and her horse followed the others.

Riding out of the forest, she felt naked with no trees around her, with no cloak of leaves over her, only the bare nighttime sky.

"Better leave the horses here," she said as they passed one last copse of trees.

"Aw! You just don't like horsies," Etty teased.

"You're right." Ro eyed her. "But a beggar boy on horseback—don't you think that would make the guards look twice?"

They did as Ro said and continued on foot. The horses had served them well, getting them to Nottingham before the gates closed.

They entered without being noticed, for the town was swarming with people. Market day? Ro wondered. Or had this great crowd all gathered for the sake of seeing Robin Hood hang at dawn? Her shoulders tightened, her back felt sweaty cold, her stomach clenched at the thought. Sweet Robin with his droll smile. Her father. And she had not told him.

"It's just off the square, where they're keeping him," she heard a loud country fellow declare to his wife.

Ro and Etty and Lionel followed the crowd. A knot of gawking folk had gathered outside a tall wattle-and-timber building like a guild hall, only larger, with dwelling space over the great room. From within, Ro heard noisy talk and much laughter. Blazing torchlight shone out of the partially open door.

"Is he up there?" asked the country wife, peering at the small windows under the steep shingle roof.

"Nah! You ninny! They'll have him shackled in the dungeon." The man jerked his chin toward a windowless wing of the building off to the left.

"Lionel," Ro whispered.

He turned to her, nodding—it was time. "I've never sung in a hall," he said, although not in his usual plaintive tone.

He had a right to be frightened, Ro knew. Through the door she could see the men slurping rowdily at their flagons of frothing ale. The big, guffawing one larded with gold might have been the sheriff. And—*Oh, Lady help me,* Ro thought. She saw a glimpse of black horsehide. Guy of Gisborn.

"I'd better not sing any lays of Robin Hood," Lionel added, trying to joke.

"You don't need them," Ro told him softly. "You remember the first day I met you? Night, rather. When you sang in the forest, and the—the denizens—"

"I remember."

The night when the world had stopped to listen to him. "Sing like that," Ro said. "Only better."

"Whatever you say, my dear fellow." He rolled his eyes at her, then turned away, unslung his harp from his shoulder and strode toward the door of the sheriff's barracks hall.

"Now," Ro whispered to Etty.

She just nodded. She was very brave, Ro realized, to be doing this for a person she barely knew. What might happen to her if she were caught? But so far no one in the crowd had noticed them. The liveried men-at-arms stationed outside the sheriff's hall had been too busy looking at the dairymaids standing with their country-awkward mothers and fathers and brothers; the dairymaids had been too busy looking at courtly squires with curling hair, at sooty-faced tinkers and lanky journeymen and velvet-hatted merchants and town tarts with a scandalous hint of red tincture on their lips. And now they were all too busy listening to the music—music such as they might not hear again in their lifetimes. To anyone who cared to glance their way, Ro and Ettarde were just two skinny boys worming their way toward the front of the crowd. Trying to get closer to the minstrel. Like everyone else.

Like the guards, even.

The guards had come out to hear the minstrel.

The guards had opened the prison door and stood in the doorway, with their backs to their duty. They might have been flogged had the sheriff seen them, but they could not help themselves; they stood there listening with their mouths open.

"By the Lady," Etty murmured, her eyes widening and her steps slowing as Lionel swept into a ballad of King Arthur, as his voice carried the song away like coursers, soared like falcons, as the harp notes rang like swords and bluebells, flew like skylarks. "By the Lady." Etty faltered to a halt. Ro took her by the hand and tugged her to get her moving again. Having heard Lionel sing before, and with her terror for Robin Hood driving her, Ro could close her ears to the music this time.

"Now," she whispered again, and she padded up the three stone steps to the prison doorway and slipped in. Between the guards. Shoulder first she edged her way between them, and Etty followed her in, and the guards moved aside and never noticed, so well had Lionel's music bound them in its spell.

Inside, dim torchlight seemed only to thicken the smoky darkness, and Ro heard a sound that made her feel cold: the slithering of chains against stone. Standing on tiptoe to see through the barred opening in the door, she looked into the first cell, and her heart turned over. The wretch shackled to the wall was barely recognizable as a man. Somebody needed to get him out of there before he died of starvation. But—but she couldn't. She couldn't save them all.

"It's not Robin," Etty whispered to her.

"Dungeon," Ro muttered, forcing herself to move on, peeking in at each prisoner she passed just long enough to be sure that none of them was Robin Hood. Lionel's singing sounded faintly through the walls. Some of the prisoners had lifted their heads, listening, and the looks on their gaunt faces made Ro want to cry.

She came to narrow stone stairs and ventured down to where—

Oh, Lady have mercy. The sight of the other prisoners prepared Ro somewhat for seeing Robin Hood there, but not enough. She had known that they would have beaten him, but nothing . . . nothing could brace her for that sight.

Within the dungeon cell Robin lay on short, moldy straw, shackled, his fair hair soaked brown with blood, his clothing mottled with blood. One arm sprawled at an awkward angle—broken. But it was the way his blue eyes had clouded that clutched at Ro's heart. He lay staring up at the shadows yet seemed to see nothing.

The heavy door was fastened with a padlock. Ro pulled out her knife and struck at it with the hilt. But she was not nearly strong enough to break it.

"Not that way," Etty whispered, taking the knife out of her hand. She forced the point of the blade into the padlock's keyhole as far as it would go, then shook her head. "Do you have something narrower?"

Ro opened the pocket on the side of her quiver and showed Etty the supplies in there: horsehair, hemp and a sturdy needle for repairing bowstrings and fletching arrows.

"Good," Etty whispered. She took the needle and thrust it into the lock. She probed, a faraway look in her eyes.

"Is this one of the things a princess learns to do?" Ro asked under her breath.

"Shhh. Yes. But not from tutors." There was a click, and the padlock dropped open.

Ro wrestled it out of its iron loop, heaved open the heavy door and ran in, dropping to her knees on the stone floor beside Robin Hood. "Robin," she whispered.

He blinked and turned his clouded gaze to her. His eyes widened in mild surprise at seeing her there, looking down on him. "Angels," he mumbled.

"No. It's Rowan and . . ." Ro stopped short of saying Ettarde's name. Her hands fumbling with haste, she pulled four arrows from her quiver and cut off the heads and the feathering, letting the pieces drop to the floor. She grabbed an extra bowstring and shifted position so that she could bind the arrow shafts as a makeshift splint around Robin's broken arm. Etty was at work with the needle on his shackles; already she had one of them open.

"Angels," Robin insisted, his voice weak. "I hear angels singing. Am I dying already?"

"No," Rowan told him. "It's Lionel. You hear Lionel."

He gazed back at her without comprehension.

"Is he going to be able to walk?" Etty asked, strain in her voice.

"He'll have to. Robin, here." Ro searched among the supply of herbs in her pouch, found the packet she wanted and pulled it out. "Robin. Eat this. Quickly." When he did not move to obey her, she put her finger in the corner of his mouth, pried it open and spilled the stuff in.

He gulped, gagged, gulped again. The other shackle gave way with a snap, and at the sound Robin startled like a deer and sat up. There was pain in his eyes now, but he was awake. "Rowan, lad?" he said as if he had not seen her before.

"Yes. Get up." Rowan and Ettarde helped him up, one on each side of him. He wobbled at first, then stood more strongly as the dose Ro had given him took effect. "Good," she whispered to him. "Let's get you out of here."

"How?" Etty murmured. "If they see us——"

But there was no time to answer, for there came the sound of heavy booted footsteps on the stone stairs. Letting Robin stand on his own, Rowan strung her bow and nocked an arrow as the footfalls approached and the cell door swung open. It sounded like one man only, but that was one too many.

It was, indeed. Looming in black horsehide, Guy of Gisborn stood looking at them.

Fourteen

ah," said Guy of Gisborn. Inside the blind black horse-face over his head, his voice boomed as if in a cave. "I knew it." Lionel's singing still wafted sweet as honey, his harping as heady as wine, but Guy of Gisborn seemed not to hear. Of course he would be the one man in Nottingham untouched by the music's spell. He had no heart to touch. "So here's the bold woods-brat and—by my beard, is that the missing princess?" In the shadow of his black horse-head showed a flash of white teeth grinning. Yet he did not raise the alarm. He preferred to stand there and gloat.

"Get back," Ro said, taking a step forward, her elf-bolt aimed at his heart. This arrow could pierce his black armor.

"Bah. You wouldn't dare." He sneered, but his

glance shifted for a moment to her short flint-tipped bolt, and his leer stiffened. "Elf-sprout," he said, his voice hoarse and hollow. He recoiled as if he had seen a serpent. "Witch-brat. I will kill you."

Robin spoke, his voice quiet and clear. "Let these two go, Guy of Gisborn. I will fight you, even beaten as I am."

Gisborn's sneer returned. "Pretty Robin, are your feathers broken?"

"Just give me a weapon—"

"No. You're gallows meat, Robin Hood." Drawing his sword, crouching and inching his feet through the dungeon's dirty straw, Guy of Gisborn advanced on Ro.

She knew she had to kill him. To save herself. To save Robin.

But—it was an enormity. The memory of her mother's charred body flickered in her mind. Death was forever. She did not want to kill anyone. Not even such a man as this one.

He crept close, closer, glaring at her as if she were a viper. She pressed her lips together, she pressed her weight into the bow. Her shoulders ached, her fingers trembled on the string, she knew she had to let her bolt go. Soon. Quickly. Now—

Something whistled and blurred in the air, but it was not her arrow. Something thunk-clanked hard into the back of Guy of Gisborn's head, and his sword fell from his hand and clattered on the stone floor. He fell forward with a thud and lay still.

Etty dropped the shackles on top of him. "Come on," she whispered between her teeth. "I hate this place." She strode out the dungeon door.

Robin followed her, wobbling, and Ro followed Robin, her bow and arrow in her trembling hand, her shoulders trembling. "Thank you," she whispered to Etty.

"Hush."

Up the stone stairs—Ro and Ettarde steadied Robin, but once they reached the courtyard level he said, "I can manage now." He straightened and turned toward the doorway, his gaze rapt. "The music," he murmured.

"Yes." Ro looked at him in the torchlight. He stood strongly, as if the music helped him as much as her herbs.

"It's an angel," he said. "It has to be."

"It's Lionel."

"Who?"

"The harmless ninny." Despite Lionel's spell, Ro's

shoulders crawled with every breath. What if Guy of Gisborn got up and came after them? They had to get Robin out, they had to chance it. In the nighttime light he looked like a dirty common fellow, his fair hair darkly matted. She wished they had a hat for him to hide the hair and shadow his face, but if wishes were horses, beggars would ride. "You look like a tavern rat," she told him.

"Do I, indeed? How nice."

"With a broken arm?" Etty complained.

"Certainly. Absolutely, my dear little lad," Ro mimicked Lionel. "Come on." She turned, stiffened her flinching shoulders and led the way out of the prison.

The guards had drifted down the steps from the doorway, drawn by the music of the minstrel. The great crowd that had gathered to see Robin Hood hanged now stood in the courtyard, hushed and gazing at nothing but dreams, as Ro and Robin and a dirty beggar boy named Etty walked down the prison steps and turned toward the gates.

"By my troth," Robin whispered, lagging as the music pulled at him. "The harmless ninny, is it?" Without replying, Ro tugged him onward, into the crowd, where they had to push their way past a very tall man—

"By my troth," breathed another voice, a deep voice from the tall outlaw dressed in common yeoman's clothing. Little John. Agawk at Robin.

After one glimpse, Ro walked past without looking at Little John again, her heart clenched with fear that someone might notice his surprise. Confound this crowd—it hid them somewhat but it went on too long, seemingly forever, out of the town square and into the streets, and now Ro was looking at every face they passed, and some of them she knew. The outlaw who had told her Robin was captured. The short outlaw named Much. The one Robin had drubbed at quarterstaff play, Will Scathelock. And other outlaws mingling in the crowd. All of them, just like the peasants gathered for the hanging, standing rapt as Lionel sang.

Finally the music faded, the crowd thinned, and Ro dared to look over her shoulder. Robin walked close behind her, and she could tell by the gray look in his eyes that his strength was starting to fail. Etty walked beside him, pattering along on her bare feet with her ragged, oversized tunic fluttering around her knees.

No one else.

"Only a little farther," Ro told Robin.

He gave her a quizzical look and a hint of his

wide, warm smile. On his bruised and bloodied face it wrenched her heart. "Is that so?" He knew it was quite a bit farther to Sherwood Forest. "How do we pass the gates, my good lad?"

Ro felt her own pulse throbbing in her throat like a rabbit's, terrified, because she did not know.

The guards lounged atop the gatehouse, looking bored.

There seemed to be no choice but to see what a brash hello would do. "You up there!" Ro called.

A guard glanced down at her. "You down there," he mocked. Ro decided not to notice his mockery. In cheerful country tones she requested, "Open the gate, would you? We need to go out."

The guard peered at her as if someone had presented him with a new sort of pet. "Now, what do you think we close the gates at night for?" he inquired. "Is it because you are supposed to go out? Why, no. It's because you're not supposed to."

"But we need to get home!" Ro cried. Let him think she was a child, a simpleton. The more piteous, the better.

But he seemed a stranger to pity. "Sure, you can go home," he said. "At sunup. After they hang Robin Hood."

Dear Lady, what if he looked at Robin? He was

likely to think that Robin should be doing the talking. "But we don't have anywhere to stay!" Ro babbled. "Father got drunk and spent all our money and——"

"There's streets enough," the guard said, turning away from her.

"Open up," ordered a different voice. "Now." In the shadow behind the corner of the nearest house stood Little John, his bow drawn—a yew bow as long as he was tall, stronger than he was strong, with a clothyard shaft fit to pierce right through a man and out the other side, its honed steel tip pointed at the guard.

All of the guards stood willow-still atop the gates, and in a moment Ro saw why. Little John's was not the only bow drawn. At the corners of all the houses nearby stood other archers, the outlaws Little John had gathered from the crowd. A score of strong bowmen, the feathers of their shafts pulled back clear to their ears, a score of razor-edged arrowheads glinting in the torchlight. If the guards moved, they would be dead guards within a heartbeat.

"Never mind," Little John added, offhand. "We'll get it ourselves. Rowan, lad, you can undo those gates, can't you?"

Etty was already there, trying to lift the heavy

129

timber bar, and Ro joined her. Together they heaved it up and spread the gates wide. "Come on, Father," Ro called to Robin, her throat squeezing like a hug as she said the word.

Fifteen

S hhh," Ro told Robin, one hand on the middle of his chest to hold him down. "Lie still." With her other hand she soaked a rag torn from her leg wrappings in the cold water of the rowan-hollow spring and laid it against his bruised face.

"But—there's fighting . . ." He was still struggling to get up. Feverish and not quite rational, he was nevertheless plentifully stubborn.

"Yes, there's fighting." All had been a midnight-black bewilderment of fleeing and fighting since they had left Nottingham: getting Robin to the horses or, rather, the horses to Robin, while Little John and the other outlaws battled the guards not far behind them, then riding through the night and hearing other hoof-beats closing in on them and slipping off the horses and letting them gallop away with the pursuit after them. And feeling their way in the darkness up the rocks to the rowan hollow, half carrying Robin . . .

Now, in the first steely light of dawn, Sherwood Forest echoed with shouts and the clang of swords and the clatter of quarterstaffs. The din had awakened Robin Hood.

He tried to push Ro's hand away from his chest, but he did not have the strength. "Let me up," he said, the words coming out a feeble murmur. "I must—I must join my men—"

Lying at the other end of the hollow, awakened from not nearly enough sleep, Ettarde lifted her head and grumbled, "Robin, for the love of mercy, you're so weak that Ro can hold you down with a finger. You have a broken arm, broken ribs—"

Robin was mumbling, "—must protect you—"

"Who's protecting whom?" asked Etty sweetly.

"We have Tykell to protect us," Ro told Robin, trying to soothe him. It eased her heart to see the wolf-dog curled up at Etty's feet, ears pricked, grinning and panting.

"Assuredly. Lick the sheriff to death," he muttered, shifting his body, trying to get away from her restraining hand.

"Lie still. You'll ruin the boneset." She had placed his broken arm in a kind of gruel made of the bone-setting plant. Once it hardened around the limb, it would comfort the arm during healing better than any splint could, but it took several hours to set. Back in Celandine's grove, Ro would have dug a trough in the ground for the boneset. Here, Robin lay with his arm in just such a trough in the stone. It was as if the rowan hollow had been made for healing, spring and all.

Robin was still squirming. Ro scolded, "Lie still, toads take it!"

"Toads?" Robin mumbled, his eyebrows bewildered.

A man's roar of terror sounded not far away, and Robin jumped; Ro felt him stiffen under her touch. Tykell rose to his feet, growling. Etty sat up.

"Hush, all of you," Ro said, although her own heart beat hard and she seemed to hear that scream still echoing. "No one will come near us. Etty, do you see them, too?" Ro had not wanted to speak of what she had noticed at dawn's first light—it was too eerie, and it made her chest ache with longing. And with fear, also, although she could not say why she was afraid, or of what. Fear that they might speak, perhaps. That they might say things—things she did not want to hear.

"See whom?" Etty asked.

"Between the rowans."

Etty looked, and from the way her slim body grew profoundly still, Ro could tell that she saw. Robin could not sit up and look, but oddly, he grew still also.

"See what?" he whispered.

"The forest loves you, Robin," Ro told him tenderly. Silvered in the early light, mists rose between the rowans, the breath of earth issuing out of the hollow hills as pillars of slowly swirling light—and the mists had form. Warrior shoulders. Warrior swords. They stood with their backs to the hollow, ringing it, and Ro felt humbly grateful that they did not turn, that she did not have to look upon their proud, fierce faces, ageless faces that she remembered from another forest, a firelit night when Lionel had played the harp, singing for them.

"Guardians," she whispered to Robin, her hand on his chest where it could feel the beating of his heart, her gaze on the silver emanations of the rowan grove. "The forest has given us guardians. Nothing can harm us. Go to sleep, Robin."

When she felt his breathing steady and grow deep and even, she looked down at him. His eyes were closed. As if remembering a dream, she recalled how angry she had been at him, when his sense of fun had made him trick her the day they first met. She remembered that evening spent at his camp beneath the great oak, his rough outlaw ways with his men, the demands he made of them. And now, gazing at his sweet, sleeping face, she understood in her heart why they gave him their loyalty and their obedience, why they loved him so. His demands were what gifted them all with survival. His fun-loving mischief was what gifted them all with joy.

Robin Hood, woodland hero. She lifted her hand from his chest, rubbed her own sleepless eyes and set about making a comfrey poultice for him.

"You're a wondrous healer, Rowan," Robin said to her, sitting up with his back against the stones of the rowan hollow, leaning toward her as she tied behind his neck the sling she had made for his broken arm. Now that a few days had gone by, he was looking better and feeling much more like himself.

Bright sunlight shone down through the rowans, and the shifting feathery pattern of their leaves gilded the stones. Smiling through her weariness, Ro wrapped a pad of cloth around the knot at the back of Robin's neck so that it would not gall him.

Robin said, "A king couldn't find a better healer."

"Thank you."

"No, I thank you. Why did you not tell me you were a healer, lad? I could use such a healer in my band."

Ro knelt in front of Robin to look at the sling. It seemed to fit properly. She didn't know why she had not thought of healing as her gift, had not told him. "I'm not a lad," she said, not knowing how else to answer him. The phrase had become a joke between them.

"What are you, then?" The blue spark of fun was back in Robin's eyes, she saw. It made her smile again.

She was supposed to say that she was an outlaw, but she didn't. Did she want to be in his band? No. She wanted to be his daughter, not his healer. She didn't say anything, for she knew what she wanted to say, what she had been waiting to say, and—could she?

Sitting and stitching a tunic for herself out of russet-red broadcloth Little John had given her, Ettarde looked up, then laid aside her sewing, stood up and stretched. "I'm a lad, too, aren't I, Ro?" she said with a sidelong glance that made Ro catch her breath; did Etty know her secret? She gawked at the princess. But without seeming to notice, Etty went on: "I'm going to look for Lionel." She was going to

136

leave Ro and Robin alone to talk, she meant, and Ro knew it. "Look for Lionel" had become a plaintive joke within the past few days—it meant to leave the hollow for personal reasons. Where was Lionel? Ro wished she knew. As far as Robin's outlaws could find out, the big lummox had slipped away from the sheriff's barracks in the uproar after someone had given the alarm that Robin had escaped. But no one had seen him since. And his spare clothing and cook pack still lay by Ro's spring.

As graceful as any princess in rags could ever be, Ettarde slipped over the rocks and away. It was safe to do this now. Tykell snoozed on a sunny boulder, his bushy tail over his nose. Down in Fountain Dale deer grazed. The forest had quieted. No more warlike clamor disturbed the nesting finches. The Sheriff of Nottingham had gone to sulk in his kitchen after losing Robin, and the knights and men-at-arms of Ettarde's entourage had gone their ways. They had gone to report to Ettarde's father, perhaps. Or they were fleeing his wrath, or they had fled outlaws, or perhaps—Ro shied from the thought, but really there could be only one good reason for the peace in the Sherwood, and that would be because the invaders had seen faces in the forest.

The guardians had faded away along with the clamor, no longer needed. The thought of the aelfe made Ro's skin prickle.

Yet—yet her mother had been half aelfin.

Her mother. *Use the gifts your mother gave you, daughter of Celandine.* If ever she was going to tell Robin the truth, now was the time. She sat cross-legged in front of him. "My mother was a healer," she said.

"Your mother?"

Her heart beating like wings, Ro said it. "Celandine."

"Celandine? Of Celandine's Wood?"

She nodded, watching him. But he showed nothing except happy surprise.

"But she is a seeress, folk say! I traveled all the way there once just because of the tales I had heard. I wanted to meet—" Robin broke off, peering at Ro. "You said 'was.' You told me you have no home. Has something happened to her, Rowan?"

"She—they—they came with torches. . . ." Ro had not meant to tell him about this. She swallowed hard, feeling Robin's sky-blue gaze so gentle on her that she could barely speak. "She's dead," she managed to say.

"Oh, lad." He reached out to touch her hand.

Ro had almost forgotten what it was to cry. Grief had been riding like a stone in her chest for so long that she no longer even noticed it. But at Robin's touch, all the grief in her swelled, bigger than she was, hot, molten, scalding her eyes, shaking her, flooding out. She sobbed, she hid her face in her hands, she could see nothing—but she felt Robin there with her, his one good arm gathering her in so that she could lean on his shoulder as she wept.

She quaked with sobbing, she could not stop. She felt Robin's hand trying to soothe her, gentling her hair, his arm around her shoulders. He felt woodsy solid and warm, cradling her to the hollow of his neck, his face turned toward her, his cheek against her head. It seemed impossible that he had not cared for her all those years she was growing up. Why? Why had he never come to see her, sent for her, acknowledged her in any way? He cared now, she could tell he cared. She felt him swallow hard, she felt his pain for her. He stroked her back. He held her as tenderly as if she were a girl.

"I—could not—save her," she told him, her voice muffled against his shoulder.

She felt him nod. Between bouts of weeping she told him the story—how the great folk had hated her mother, and why. How she had been gathering coltsfoot—she did not tell him that she had been wearing an apron and a frock, she did not tell him why she was not a lad, not yet. But she told him how she had felt her mother's spell of protection, and returned to the cottage to find only ashes as hot as her tears.

Finally the spasm of crying passed. She quieted, pressed against Robin's shoulder, steadying herself with his warmth awhile before she sat up and wiped her face on her sleeve.

"I'm sorry, lad," Robin said softly.

She shook her head, wondering what he meant. Was he sorry for her, or—had he loved Celandine?

She dared a look at him. His blue eyes had gone a cloudy-sky gray. He said, his voice very low, "They might try to kill you, too, Rowan. It seems that you truly are an outlaw."

And his scarred face showed what being an outlaw meant. Yet he would try to comfort a crying—boy, he still thought she was a boy; all the more reason her heart went out to him, that he did not scorn tears in a lad. Yet—why had he never been there for her before? Could she trust him?

She had to.

Her heart wanted to trust him but her mind said no. She had to have some answers from him—she could not not bear the tug-of-war going on inside her much longer. In a moment she would tell him the truth, in just a moment she would tell him everything, but she had to tell him something else first, now that he was strong enough to talk. It was important. "Robin, you must not go to Nottingham in one of your silly disguises ever again," she said. "I think she must have put a spell of protection on you, too, a kind of woods magic so that you could fool them. But now that she is dead, it is gone."

He eyed her with his fair brows raised. "You think your mother was protecting me all this time?"

"Yes."

"But—why, lad? Or rather, how?"

"When you visited her—"

"But she was not there," Robin said. "I never met her."

Sixteen

T y," Ro told the wolf-dog, "I just want to scream. Or cry. Or die. Something. I don't know what."

She had gone off into the forest, supposedly to hunt but actually to be alone with her misery so she wouldn't need to hide it—not that she could hide it anyway. Robin thought it was her grief over her mother, maybe, that made her so taut and silent, but then Etty came back to the hollow and saw. Etty kept looking anxiously at her, and Ro had to get away.

With Tykell lying at her feet, she sat on a sunny bank dotted with wild strawberries, and they did not tempt her. High above her in a hornbeam tree, a mistle thrush sang like a ranting flute. Its loud pipings did not make Ro smile. Woe, woe, it's the rain crow, folk said when they heard the mistle thrush, and Ro believed them. She felt like rain, even though there was not a cloud in the sky.

"I want my mother," she muttered, trying to jest with herself, but tears prickled at her eyes.

"Toads take it. Why would she lie?" Ro whispered to Tykell. Her heart ached at the thought. "She couldn't have." Celandine did not lie. Ro could not think of any instance when her mother had lied to her, even about something unimportant. And to tell her that her father was Robin Hood . . . "She wouldn't have. She would never have told me that unless it was true."

But that meant Robin had lied.

"He couldn't have!" The thought made Ro clutch at her own knees, curled up as if someone were hitting her. Tykell whined, stood up and licked her face. She reached for him and hugged him, hanging on to his strength, his warmth.

"I was looking right at his face when he said it. It was as clear as—" As clear as the summer day all around her. "As clear as springwater. I'd swear to anyone that he wasn't lying."

More. She would swear to anyone that Robin would never lie to her. About anything.

She would swear that he was—he was brave, ardent, gallant, true. All that the ballads said he was. And more.

"Lady help me," she murmured to Ty, "if he is not my father, then—then my mother was a liar, and I have no one."

He had to be her father. He had to be.

"Why would my mother lie?"

The questions led her only in circles. She was back where she had started. This was getting her nowhere.

She let go of the wolf-dog and pressed her hands to the sides of her own aching head. "Ty," she whispered, "I am going to go as crazed as a broken pot." The sun warmed her and the fragrance of wild strawberries rose around her knees, but it could not help her. Nothing could help her. Nothing could ease her misery.

Or so she thought.

Tykell woofed and turned to peer downhill, ears pricked, tail wagging. The loud, piping mistle thrush fell silent. And in the silence Ro heard the crashing of something, someone, a large lummox, blundering through brush down below. And a voice far sweeter than birdsong wafted to her, a voice like honey butterflies and golden falcons.

Lionel sang:

"In hidden glades of wild Sherwood
 There lives an archer fair and free,
 An outlaw bold as gold, yet good
 Of heart. Folk call him Robin Hood . . ."

"I knew it," said Etty, unsurprised by what Ro had just told her. "I knew you were a girl."

Lionel bleated, "I've been taking orders from a *girl?*"

Ignoring him, Rosemary asked Ettarde, "How did you know?"

"Because you wanted me to come to Nottingham with you. A boy would have wanted to leave me behind. And," Etty added wickedly, "because you have such good sense."

"Good sense?" Lionel complained, his feet taking up half the stone hollow as he lounged. "Sending me into the lion's den?"

"I'm so glad you're safe, Lionel. We've been worrying. Robin was worried." Robin had gone back to his band; Little John and some others had come for him while Ro was away from the hollow. But Ro expected that Robin would find some way to thank Lionel as soon as he could. She herself had already thanked the reluctant minstrel again and again, and hugged him, to his consternation. Now, while a brace of pheasants roasted over a slow fire, she was explaining to Ettarde and Lionel what was making her so miserable. Telling them the whole story, everything, both to ease her aching heart and because—because they were her friends. They might be able to help somehow. They might see something she was missing.

"That knight was there." Lionel was still complaining about his own ordeal. "The one I clobbered. I was *scared*. I was so scared I almost wet myself."

"Did he say anything?" Etty had a way of getting right to the point.

"No. He just listened to the music. But then I had to clobber him again to get away. Maybe I really did kill him this time."

Ro sighed. Too many problems. "So where have you been hiding all this time?"

"In the forest. But I couldn't hide, that was my problem! Wherever I tried to hide, parts of me stuck out. I was in *terrible danger*."

Ettarde turned to Ro elegantly, like a bored cat. "Rowan, you were trying to tell us something."

Lionel said, "Finally, those outlaw friends of yours took me into their hollow oak. You know the huge oak down in the clearing? It's hollow. A dozen men—"

"Rosemary, I mean," said Etty to Ro.

"You can call me Rowan. I like it better."

"A dozen men were staying in there," declared Lionel. "Wounded. They had bloody bandages on them. It was *dreadful*."

Etty rolled her perfect eyes. "Rowan, go on with your story. Please."

Ro did. She told them about Celandine and what had happened to her—even Lionel quieted to listen. She told them how she had journeyed to find Robin Hood—Tykell wandered in from somewhere, licked her hand and lay down at her feet. She told them about her doubts: If Robin was her father, why had he never come to see her? Was it because she was a girl? Or was he not her father after all? And if he was not—why had her mother said he was?

Twilight had turned to night and the pheasants had cooked through by the time she finished. Etty offered her browned skin and white meat on a good brown bread trencher, but Ro shook her head. "I'm not hungry."

Etty put the food down, gazing at Ro. "You know," she said softly, "Robin will always be your friend, even if he's not your father."

True.

"Having a father isn't everything. Look at what my father did to me."

But Robin was everything. All those years of dreaming. All that had sustained her on the long road to Sherwood. And now—to have a real father instead of a dream one, and he was almost better than the dream—Ro had not told Etty and Lionel how she felt about Robin Hood, how she was starting to adore him. But she did not have to. They knew.

She managed to ask Etty quietly, "You think—you think he's not my father?"

"I don't know. I don't know what to think."

In the process of eating a whole pheasant by himself, Lionel said, "Maybe you won't ever know."

Despite the way he spoke through a mouthful of fowl, he spoke gently, and he spoke truth. But it was not an easy truth to accept. Ro swallowed hard.

Ettarde asked, "Is there anyone besides your mother and Robin who would know? Grandparents?"

"No." Ro had never met her mother's parents. "They died before I was born."

But then, thinking of her mortal grandfather, her grandmother from under the hollow hills, Ro sat bolt upright, her eyes open wide.

"The aelfe," she whispered, and she began to tremble.

Seventeen

Ro returned to the place where she had first met Robin Hood, along the steep bank of a stream, where bluebells had bloomed and his handsome, astonished face had peered out of a wreath of ivy. It was the memory that pulled her there, and the bluebells, an otherworldly flower, that made her think she might find the aelfe there—though in truth she might find them anywhere, everywhere. Any morning, mists stirred and swirled when there was no breeze. They were aelfin. Most summer mornings, a starry many cobwebs covered the world, shining with dew, and anyone who had eyes could see how they quivered with life, with the breath of earth, the breath of the aelfe. The old ones were in earth itself.

This summer morning, Ro went to the streambank

alone. She wanted to take Ty with her, and Etty, and she wanted Lionel with her to sing the aelfe out of the hollow hills, but some whisper deep in her chest gave her to know that she must go alone. She had walked toward this day when she had walked alone toward Sherwood. In a way she had been walking toward this day for years.

She set out at daybreak and came to the stream a little after dawn. The bluebells and columbine were gone. Now sorrel and buttercups bloomed, just opening as the early sunrays touched them. The streambank had grown up into a thorny tangle of wild roses in bud.

Ro stood by the mossy trunk of the same great tree where she had first met Robin Hood, gazing the way she had gazed that day. Balanced on the edge of her heartache, the world seemed even more beautiful today. It was going to be a soft day, dove-colored with maybe some small rain. The sky lustered like the inside of a mussel shell, and every bird in Sherwood seemed to be singing. Ro gazed, blinking, at the sheen of dew on greenleaf, and every inch of her quivered, as watery as the dew. Watery with fear.

But she had to do it.

As if addressing the spirit of Celandine's spring or the spirit of fire or the spirit of a birch stick as she fletched it into an arrow, Ro whispered to the forest, "My kinsfolk."

Nothing happened. But Ro seemed to feel a sort of sigh, as if earth were her mother, busy with other things, and had turned to her, annoyed by her whining.

Ro tried again. "My kinsfolk, please. I need to speak with you."

The birds seemed to quiet—perhaps only because it was time for them to quiet down and get on with feeding, but Ro trembled harder.

"My kinsfolk," she whispered a third time, "will you speak to me? I need to ask you something."

Her mind wished the aelfe to speak, but her fearful heart did not. She startled like a deer when the voice asked her, "What is wrong, daughter of Celandine?"

She jumped and looked everywhere, for the voice came from everywhere, from the oak, the stream, the wild roses, the earth, the sky. But chiefly it came from in front of her, from a pillar of shimmering air with a face made of mist and dayspring light.

A face she knew well, droll smile and all. Ro felt her knees go weak. She had to press one hand against the oak for support.

"Robin?" she breathed.

"Robin Hood is resting in the oak glade," the voice said. "Yet he is here. And you are here. Yet you are at the rowan grove as well, are you not, daughter of Celandine?"

The face made of air and light rippled like fire and water. And there were no scars on it, no half-healed cuts. And its eyes were not blue and bright, but heather-gray and fey. It was Robin—yet it was not. "I—I don't understand." Ro felt her eyes go stinging hot; there was so much she did not understand and she felt so much the child. "I just want to know who my father is." She just wanted to get this over with.

"Use the gifts your mother gave you."

As we told you before, the tone of the voice said. A voice not male, not female. The rustling of oak leaves was in it, and the whistling of mistle thrushes, and the murmur of brown streams, and the moonlit song of wolves, and the soft-eyed leaping of roes. Ro trembled like a deer.

The gifts her mother gave her? Her mother had given her love, mostly. And life. And from her mother she had inherited the gift for finding sweet-water. Nothing else.

"Please," Ro said, "I don't understand. Please, just tell me. Who is my father?"

"But you know who your father is."

She wanted to stamp her foot and scream. She wanted to shoot something. She wanted to cry. She stood there.

"You will never understand," the voice said, "until you answer this: Of what are you so afraid?"

I am not afraid! Ro wanted to shout. But her answer must be honest to the core, the whisper in her chest told her. "Of you. Of course I am afraid," she said, her voice low. Who would not be afraid of the aelfe?

"But why?"

"You—you drove out my grandmother, my mother—"

"We drove no one out. They changed, like the wind changes, and we let them be. Sometimes the falcon returns to the falconer. Sometimes not."

Ro blinked, gazing hard at the swirling, strange and familiar face of light before her. Somehow she found the strength to speak utmost truth.

"I am afraid of being a woodwife like my mother," she said.

"As might well happen," the voice agreed dryly.

Now Ro's eyes stung like scorched stones; she could not have cried if she tried. "I will live my life alone?"

"That is up to you."

"I—they will come to kill me? As they did her?"

"Perhaps. But have they killed her, really? Use the gifts she gave you, daughter of Celandine." The aelfe faded away.

Her legs wobbling, her knees folding under her, Ro clung to the oak and slipped down to sit at its base. She laid her head against the deep, random pattern of its bark and closed her eyes, paying attention only to the images within her mind. She sat that way for a long time.

Wuff.

Blinking, Ro opened her eyes as Tykell bounded up to her, panting and grinning. She smiled, sat up and hugged him around his shaggy neck. One side of her face felt red-ridged from lying against the oak tree.

"There you are, Rowan, lad!" Slipping between the tangles of wild roses without, seemingly, being touched by a thorn, Robin Hood strode up to her. Tykell settled himself on the ground, his furry back pressed against her leg, as Robin squatted to peer at her. "They told me I'd find you here." Robin sat down beside her, perhaps because he was tired. He looked pale, as if his arm might be hurting him.

Ro lost her smile. "You shouldn't be gadding about," she told him. "You're not strong enough yet."

"I wanted to thank you."

"You already did."

"No. I never thanked you properly." He leveled his gaze at her, stark earnest—she had never seen his eyes so serious yet shining blue. "Rowan, I keep thinking about—about lying there in that filthy dungeon, and hearing angels, and expecting to die, and then I was looking up and—and seeing angels, too. You and Ettarde. I think about it all the time, I see it in my dreams but I still can't believe it. What you did—"

Ro interrupted, because his thanks were clotting her chest, lumping in her throat. "Your men would have saved you anyway."

"They would have tried, but they could not have done it half as well. And many of them would have died for trying. But my men are sworn to me; you're not. That's why I keep shaking my head. I can't get past the wonder of it. Why am I alive, lad?"

"I'm not a lad," Ro told him. Her voice came out quiet and shaky.

"You're right, you're not. You're an outlaw, brave and true."

Ro took a deep breath and laid a hand on Ty for steadiness. She said, "Yes. And I'm a girl."

Watching him, she saw his mouth drop open, his eyes fly open wide as he gawked, every bit as astonished as he had been that first day, when Ty had snatched his bolt out of the air—but then, as he found his breath, his gawk turned to a grin wider than his eyes.

"A girl!" he exclaimed. "Of course. I should have known it before. You make a fine, straight arrow of a girl."

Her heart beating hard, Ro managed to say, "You don't mind?"

"Mind? Hardly. Rowan, you're no less a wonder for being a girl."

"You said—you said a girl had no place in the greenwood—"

"It would seem I was wrong." He said this as if it were a treat for him to be wrong. Smiling. Eyes alight.

"You—you think I can be an outlaw. . . ."

"Rowan, you *are* an outlaw."

Now.

Ro lifted her hand from Ty and laid it instead on her own chest. Under her palm, and under her jerkin, resting next to her heart, she could feel a quiet circle of silver. The one other gift her mother had given her, she had remembered. The one other inheritance.

Her voice as quiet and silver as if she were aelfe speaking, she said, "Robin—I'm your daughter."

And she understood now why he had never acknowledged her. He didn't know.

He gasped. He stared at her without speaking, without breathing.

"When you went to see my mother," she told him, "she was there. Always, she was there."

He struggled for breath before he spoke. "The fire—a fire waited for me on the hearth. But—there was no one—"

"She was the fire on the hearth, she was the light in the air, she was the water in the spring and the earth under your head when you lie down. She had those powers." Ro found that she was trembling again when she spoke of these things. For comfort, she slipped her mother's gimmal ring out of her jerkin, holding it in her hand. Robin's glance dropped to the bright glint of silver, and he stiffened.

"Let me see that," he demanded.

Startled by his tone, Ro looked at him.

"Please." His voice had gone hoarse.

She slipped the string over her head and handed him the many-stranded ring. He turned it over and over, then sat staring at it. Ro curled her arms around her own shaking knees and kept silent.

"I thought it was a dream," Robin whispered. He looked at her, his eyes like blue butterflies in sunlight. "I could have sworn I slept through the night—but she was real, wasn't she? She wore this. And she wore green."

"Yes," Ro said. Celandine always wore green.

"She was so beautiful. . . ." Robin let his voice trail away. With a wavering hand he gave the ring back to her. "Rowan—I mean—is that truly your name?"

"Yes. It is now." It was her true name. She wanted him always to call her Rowan.

"By the Lady," he breathed, "Rowan. A daughter." He gazed at her. "I've never had family. I never expected . . ." His voice faltered to a halt. Ro saw tears well up in his bright eyes and flow down his bruised cheeks.

"Robin, don't cry. Please, don't." On her knees, she reached for him and hugged him. He embraced her with his one good arm, his head on her shoulder. "I'm your daughter," she told him, stroking his fair hair. "I'm your family. And that's why you don't have to thank me for anything, idiot." Tears rippled in her voice. "I'm your daughter, and I love you."

Eighteen

W ill you go stay with him now?" Etty asked.

Giving the spit a turn to evenly roast a haunch of venison over the fire, Rowan shook her head. "He asked me to join his band." More than once Robin had asked her. "But I can't. Or—I don't understand me, but—I don't want to. I belong here now." Sitting back on a ledge of mossy stone, Ro gestured, her gimmal ring flashing in the late-day light—she wore it on her finger now. She opened her hands to include everything: the spring, the stones, the rowan grove ringing the rocky hollow, the forested crags all around. A deep gladness glowed in her heart, a feeling as warm and golden as the sunlight—she had a father and a home. "I belong here the way my mother belonged in her wood, her glade." Rowan's voice grew softer. "And that frightens me. A little."

Etty nodded, a simple tilt of the head that showed she understood most of what Ro was not saying. "Well, you won't be alone," Etty said, her tone as peaceful as the sunset gilding Sherwood Forest— Ettarde hardly ever seemed less than peaceful, even when she was conking Guy of Gisborn. "You have Tykell." The wolf-dog dozed near the fire. "And me. I'll stay with you, if that's agreeable to you."

Of course it was. More than agreeable. So much more that Ro smiled as wide as a sunlit sky but could not speak.

"Don't take any account of me," Lionel complained, stretched across most of the hollow. "I'll be around, is that agreeable? Isn't that meat ever going to be ready? I'm hungry."

Rowan turned to look at the venison just in time to see it lift off the fire, spit and all, then disappear over the rocks. She caught just a glimpse of a thin brown hand vanishing behind a plume of rowan leaf.

"Hey!" she yelled, leaping up, snatching her bow and arrows as she ran after her dinner. Ty was ahead of her, dashing over the rocks with a woof, then charging up the steep hillside between the crags.

Trusting her dog's nose for both venison and trouble, Ro followed.

The thief did not go far. Halfway up the slope, Ro found him backed into a shallow cave under the crags, crouching, tearing at the burning-hot meat with his fingers and teeth, gulping it by the handful. His hollow cheeks shiny with grease, he stared at her over the meat and bolted it faster. His dark eyes glared huge from his starved face, like black coals burning.

Rather than snarling at him, Ty whined. Ro sighed and unstrung her bow. "You could have asked," she told the boy as Etty and Lionel came panting up behind her. "We would have given you some."

The dark boy continued to tear at the meat and did not answer. He wore no jerkin, and hot venison fat smeared his bare, ribby chest. Ro guessed he was about her age, although he looked small because he was so thin. Only his black hair grew thick, clotted over his burning eyes like a wild pony's mane.

"What's your name?" Rowan asked.

He did not answer. He savaged the meat, dropping scraps at his thin, bare feet. Tykell gobbled the scraps, then licked drippings off the boy's shins.

"It's nice that somebody's getting fed," Lionel hinted.

"Oh, for mercy's sake, Curlylocks," Etty told Lionel, "hush. It wouldn't hurt you to miss a meal or two."

Ro said to the boy, "You've burned your hands. Come—there's water at the hollow, and poultice, and bread to eat."

For the first time he stopped bolting meat. He sat where he was and stared at her.

"Come, eat with us," she said again, and she turned and walked away. Etty walked with her. Lionel hesitated.

"Lionel," Ro told him, "come on."

"Our supper," he begged.

"Lionel."

He followed. He said nothing more until they got back to the hollow, and then he said only, "I don't understand."

Busy searching her pouch for a remedy for burns, Ro did not answer.

"I don't bloody understand why I do what you say," said Lionel in tones of honest bewilderment. "I could have taken that haunch away from him—"

Etty shushed him by lifting one placid hand. "Here it comes," she told him, "your precious supper."

The dark boy scrambled over the lip of the hollow, carrying what was left of the haunch, and placed the spit back on the forked sticks that had held it over the fire. He turned as if to leave, but Ro stopped him with one hand on his shoulder. "Sit down."

As she washed his burned face and chest and hands with cool springwater she asked once again, "What is your name?"

He still didn't answer, only watched her with his dark eyes.

"Maybe he's mute," Lionel said. Ro noticed that Lionel had not touched the venison or the loaves of bread wrapped in dock leaves that Etty was lifting from the hot ashes.

Rowan smoothed a paste made of crushed elder bark onto the stranger boy's burns, sat down, took a hunk of bread for herself and offered some to the boy. He took it from her, but cautiously, hesitating like a half-tamed fox pup. Ro sighed and chewed a hunk of warm, fresh bread. "Eat something, Lionel," she said gently.

He shook his head and brought out his harp instead. He struck a few notes softly. Comfort rang through the rowan grove.

The boy turned to him, wide-eyed. "You're that outlaw minstrel!" His voice was soft and low-pitched, with a hint of a burr.

Lionel missed a note and peered at him. "Am I outlawed indeed?"

"If I could take your head to the Sheriff of Nottingham right now, he'd be honor bound to give me a hundred pounds of gold." The boy's tone indicated that he did not much trust the sheriff's honor. His glance touched Etty, then Rowan. "He has promised gold for any one of you. But more likely he'd give me death." The quiet, velvety way he said it touched Ro like a finger to her spine.

"So we're all outlaws." Lionel said it just as quietly, stroking comfort out of his harp again. "You, too."

The boy did not answer. His silence gave the answer.

Ro gazed down at her own hands, fingering the gimmal ring, noting how its many strands glowed silver in twilight, golden in firelight. She pulled it off her hand and held it up, catching the light for the others to see.

"Look," she said, "a band."

Lionel silenced his harp to look at her. Etty looked at her. The dark, silent boy whose name she did not yet know watched her.

"A ring is a band," Rowan said. "A circle of many strands is a band. We are a band. An outlaw band."

Lionel spoke almost as if he were singing. "And you are our leader."

"No." Rowan shook her head. "Look." Holding

the ring high in both hands, she pulled it apart, then puzzled the many strands together again. "Which is the leader?"

Silence. Then Etty said softly, "They're all part of the band."

"I think so." Ro spoke slowly, choosing her words with care. "Any one of them—us—could stand alone. But together—" Her thoughts faltered, for this idea was a great newness sunrising in her, blooming like dayspring seemingly from the oaks and rowans and rocky hills and mists rising and dew beaded bright on fern fronds, springing like sweetwater from earth itself. It felt fitting yet vast—she could not yet see it all clearly. "Together—we make a strong, shining thing." She lowered her hands slowly, holding the ring in one palm, gazing beyond it to Etty, Lionel, the wolf-dog lying by the spring and the dark stranger looking back at her.

"Daughter of Robin Hood," Lionel said quietly, sounding as formal as Ettarde at her very stateliest, "I would be honored to swear fealty to you."

The dark boy stiffened, staring at her, Robin Hood's daughter. Ro did not answer his stare. She wanted no such title. "If you must swear to something," she told Lionel just as quietly, "swear to the ring."

"But you wear the ring."

"No." Rowan got up. With a strange sureness guiding her, as if she were feeling across the distance of time and death her mother's blessing, she separated the silver strands of the ring in the palm of her hand. There were half a dozen strands in all. One she gave to Ettarde, who accepted it with quiet serenity and placed it on her own finger. One she offered to Lionel, who accepted it far more hesitantly, then fumbled it onto a tunic lacing, wearing it over his heart.

And one of the silver rings Ro offered to the dark boy, the stranger, but he shook his head. "I have not yet earned it," he said.

"How long have you been living in your cave? How long have you known we were here?" Rowan asked him.

"Many days."

"And you have not betrayed us." Rowan stated this as a fact.

But he answered anyway. "No. Why should I?"

She told him, "You have earned your strand of the band."

He thought, then nodded and accepted it from her, easing it onto a finger of his burned hand.

Rowan replaced the three remaining strands on her own finger. "Come," she said to the giant minstrel and the placid princess and the silent, wolfish boy sitting nearby, "make a circle around the spring. Join hands. We will all swear fealty—to each other."

"Nevertheless, they swore to you," Robin Hood remarked.

Rowan gave him a quizzical look. Sitting on the sunny rocks over the spring, trying to tell him about her band, she found herself not explaining very well. It was too sweet and motherly a day, smiling with white and yellow butterflies, sun warming her shoulders through her new jerkin of soft doeskin, heart warm with love of her father, and she did not have the heart to say anything that might shadow him even for a moment. So she had not explained very well that she would not let anyone swear obedience to her, or that no one had to best her in anything to be one with her in the band. She did not want him feeling her ways as a judgment on his. She was just different than he was, that was all, and her band was different than his, and it might do different things. Her band might somehow help folk to help themselves, Rowan thought, rather than just giving them gold stolen from rich men's packs, gold soon spent. But she could not say that, for she loved everything about Robin Hood. It was just that her dreams flew a different way than his. And today the rowan trees were budding, soon to flower into white blossom, and butterflies were flying and the skylarks singing and it was too bright-eyed a day for these things.

"Younglings," Robin said with a quirk in his voice. "What a harsh world we live in." His broken arm and scarred, still-healing face showed that he knew of the world's harshness, but he was not speaking of himself. "Younglings wandering the wild woods with nowhere else to go. Two lads and a lass giving their fealty to another brave lass."

"They swore to the ring," Rowan told him, "not to me."

"They swore to the ring and the spring," Robin said, "and so they swore to you, Rowan. This place—it is you." His voice went very low, struggling to say what Rowan herself sensed but would not say, that she was in the rocks and the sweetwater and the rowan grove and they were in her. Robin could not say it, but only lifted his head, scanning the green plumes of rowan leaf with his azure gaze. "I like rowan trees," he said softly. "They're slim and small, but they're tough and they'll grow anywhere. They take root in stony soil. They're a mystic tree. Diviners use rowan to find precious metal. And they are beautiful." He looked at her, his blue eyes serious for once,

telling her without words that he found her beautiful also.

"They make good firewood, too," Ro said, trying
to lighten the moment.

"No, they don't." Robin looked at her again, shook
his head in a wondering way and stood up. "Rowan—
I'll always be nearby if you need me."

She stood up also and hugged him, laying her
head for a moment against his warm, solid shoulder.
He returned the hug as best he could with his good
arm.

"And you, I suppose," he added, "will always be
nearby if I need you."

She grinned.

Beyond him, beyond the rowan grove, Ro could
see Etty practicing with her new bow and arrow,
learning to shoot. Tykell was catching the arrows and
bringing them back to her. The dark boy who still
would not tell anyone his name was walking up the
hill with a pouch full of perch for supper—Ro did
not understand how he did it, but he seemed to catch
fish with his bare hands. Someday, she promised herself, she would know his story and she would understand him better.

And Lionel. Someday she would know more of Lionel's story. The big brave-hearted complaining oaf.

He sat in the hollow plucking out shreds of melody on his harp, trying to put together a new song.

"They will be singing of you after I'm dead and gone, Rowan," said Robin.

"No, they won't." She did not like to think that he would ever be gone.

"Yes, they will," said Robin Hood with a merry blue glance, with a wide, warm smile. "Listen."

Lionel's song came wafting up, and in it Ro heard butterflies and skylarks and oak shadows and river-sheen and the midnight running of wolves. The song rose like hawk flight, like fern fronds, like swirling mists out of bluebells and columbine:

> *"In a hollow hill of wild Sherwood*
> *There lives a maiden brave and free*
> *With a wolf who gives her fealty.*
> *Daughter of fitting fatherhood*
> *An archer with a healer's hand*
> *A shining strand in an outlaw band*
> *This maiden outlaw bold and good,*
> *Rowan Hood of the rowan wood."*

TURN THE PAGE FOR A PREVIEW
OF NANCY SPRINGER'S NEXT
ROWAN HOOD BOOK:

Lionclaw

A TALE OF ROWAN HOOD

One

Trudging through Sherwood Forest, with his harp nestled like a turtledove in one big hand, Lionel did not even try to be quiet. It was no use. His feet, the size of pony heads in their curly-tipped shoes, would never learn not to scrape and shuffle. His great lumbering body would never learn not to rustle brush and bracken. And his poor muddled head, seven feet above the ground, would never learn not to conk itself on tree limbs. He made a poor excuse for an outlaw, forsooth.

According to his father, he made a poor excuse for a son altogether.

Lionel slowed, gazing up at tall oaks with acorns fattening on their branches, their autumn leaves hanging muted purple, like old royal velvet, in the twilight. Somewhere high in the darkening sky wild geese bayed like hounds, but Lionel barely heard. Instead, he heard

1

in memory his father's voice: "You disgrace my name. My heir, a sissy, a harp plucker? You are no son of mine. Go. If I see you again, I will kill you."

The words echoed in Lionel's mind. Yes, kill. His father had really said that.

And meant it. Lionel remembered his father's eyes narrowed to slits above his beard, remembered the lion growl in his father's voice. A great lord can, and will, kill whomever he pleases.

My father.

Two years ago he had threatened Lionel with death. *On my birthday.* Thirteenth. Unlucky number.

Lionel sighed, lowered his gaze from the storm-purple oaks, and trudged on. In the months since another powerful man, the Sheriff of Nottingham, had put a bounty on his head, he had become accustomed to the threat of death. But remembering his father saying *You are no son of mine.* He had not yet become accustomed to the heartache.

Or the fear. He often quivered with nerves—oversized, sniveling ninny that he knew himself to be—but he had seldom felt such bone-deep terror as now.

But . . . I have to try.

He slogged on, under the oaks, along a ridge, then into thickets of hemlock and holly, their shadows deepening as night fell. Then down into a rocky dell,

2

where ferns brushed his legs, their fronds dry and yellow at this time of year. Lacework leaves as yellow as primroses, as yellow as Lionel's jerkin; yellow was his favorite color. The butter-bright ferns seemed to glow in the twilight. Gazing at them, Lionel stubbed his toe, stumbled into a boulder, and almost dropped his harp. A blackthorn branch raked his shoulder. His hand, flung out to grab something solid, found only a patch of nettles. "Owww!" he complained.

"Lady have mercy, harper," said a quiet voice in the nightfall. "A deaf man could hear you coming."

Peering into the shadows, Lionel could just make out the gleam of a polished longbow, then behind it the form of a man in green. Uphill from Lionel, motionless and almost invisible amid wild quince and ivy, one of Robin Hood's men was standing guard duty.

Lionel cringed. "Don't shoot me!" he squeaked.

In the dusk he could not see the outlaw's good-humored contempt, but he depended on it, knowing it was there. "Maybe not this time," the man said. "Are you on your way to join the feast?"

Standing still, with the ferns no longer rustling around his shins, Lionel could hear the talk and laughter of the outlaws in their hideout on the other side of the rise.

Seeming to take his silence for ignorance, the guard

3

said, "Robin has brought in a rich lord today, and a dozen of his retainers." To show those whom he robbed that he was no common cutthroat, Robin Hood spared their lives but required them to spend a night with him and his band. "We are giving them our best Sherwood Forest hospitality." Illegal venison, in other words, sauced with humiliation. "But the lord seems not to like it."

Lionel nodded and whispered, "Lord Roderick Lionclaw."

"Aye! Who told you?"

"Will Scathelock." All the outlaws were Lionel's friends, amused by his vast size and timid disposition. "He said Lionclaw fought hard."

"Harder than most, but no match for Robin Hood and his merry men."

Small wonder. Anyone who wanted to join Robin's band had to take on Robin in single combat. One of the many ironies of Lionel's life, he considered, was that he had become an outlaw by helping to save Robin Hood's life, yet he knew himself unworthy to join Robin's band.

No matter. He gave all his fealty to Rowan: Rowan Hood, daughter of Robin Hood. Without looking, Lionel could feel his strand of the band, the silver gimmal ring, hanging inside his jerkin, over his heart.

"I'm here on an errand," he told the guard.

His own errand. Still, he badly wanted not to disgrace Rowan. Or the others.

The guard nodded. Lionel blundered on.

It was almost dark now. It seemed to Lionel that he tripped over every root and stick and stone in Sherwood Forest getting to the top of the rise. But at last he reached a vantage, a crag, where he could see.

There. Robin's hollow.

Under the spreading branches of a giant oak, firelight glinted on two score grinning outlaws decked with the loot from the lord's coffers: fine swords, rich velvets, gold chains. Hoisting flagons of ale, Robin's men sat one-handedly tossing sacks of gold around the circle, roaring with laughter when they dropped the booty. Their captives, the lord's men-at-arms, sat among them, huddled like scared rabbits. Lionel could guess their thoughts: They had been defeated in battle. Their hands had been tied; they had been blindfolded and made to ride backward on their own horses, brought to this place against their will. They were not being hurt now, except for their pride, but once Robin released them, would their lord have them flogged? He had been bound and blindfolded and made to ride backward too. They did not dare to look at him.

From the safety of the trees, Lionel looked.

There. Seated in the place of mocking honor, a throne of piled deerskins near the fire, Lord Roderick Lionclaw.

Father . . .

Lionel felt his heart pounding. Had anything changed in two years? Outwardly, no. Tawny in the firelight, his father's stony face glared out over his jutting beard—the same. His broad-shouldered body, almost as tall as Lionel's, looked as powerful as ever. His hands, battered in many combats, curled as hard as claws, just the way Lionel remembered them. On his men's tabards and his own tunic gleamed Lord Roderick's device, the rampaging golden lion wielding the clawed mace that had made him famous. All the same.

Then Lionel's gaze shifted as a tall outlaw stood up, his curly cap of golden hair glinting in the firelight, his handsome, weather-tanned face alight with firelight and fun. He wore no looted gold, only his customary Lincoln green, his jaunty cap with a tuft of feathers. "Merry men, a toast!" he cried.

The others quieted, looking up to their leader, Robin Hood.

With solemn drollery Robin turned toward Lord Roderick Lionclaw, raising his flagon. "To the continued very excellent health of our honored guest."

"Hear! Hear!" the outlaws cried as Lionclaw gave Robin a glare like a blaze of dragon flame.

Robin seemed not to notice Lionclaw's fiery stare at all. "My good lord," he said in tender tones, "you have not touched your dinner. Are you not feeling well?"

Lionclaw told him, "Go to hell."

The outlaws hooted. Looking on, Lionel felt his gut tighten into a Gordian knot of mixed emotions. He knew what it was to suffer taunts. Yet as often as not, it had been his father who had taunted him.

Robin's mouth pulled down in clownish distress. "My lord is not merry? But consider, my lord, the good you have done this day! Starving peasants will be fed with the gold you have so willingly given—"

"Go fry in hell!"

Lord Lionclaw's yell echoed in the oaks and in Lionel's worst memories, making him shiver. He wanted to crawl away and hide.

I'm a fool to be here.

But—maybe not. Two years ago, when his father had cast him out, he had not known what his singing could do. He had not known that there was enchantment in his voice that could hold a guild hall full of armed men in his power, making them forget their weapons. He had not known that he could sing the badgers out of their dens, silence the nightingales,

7

coax wolf and deer to stand side by side. He had not known that the beauty of his voice could even call forth the *aelfe,* the immortal denizens of the forest, from their hollow hills to listen to him.

Maybe, just maybe, if he sang for his father . . . something might change.

Please, dear Lady, let him . . . let him hear me. . . .

His father's roar echoed away. Robin stood grinning but silent. All the men in the hollow, intent on Robin and Lionclaw, sat silent, awaiting whatever might happen next.

NOW. There would never be a better chance. *Do it!*

Shaking, Lionel set his back against an oak for support. He breathed in. Gently he touched his harp, and the first golden ringing notes quieted his trembling, made him forget the sting of nettles and mockery and hunger, made him forget his father's fury. He cradled his harp, looked out of darkness straight into his father's fiery face, stroked a strong chord out of the harp, lifted his voice, and sang:

> *"In a hollow hill of wild Sherwood*
> *There lives a maiden fair and free,*
> *An archer with a healer's hand*
> *A shining strand in an outlaw band. . . ."*

Praise be to the Lady, his voice flew true, like a golden falcon, like the fragrance of wild roses, like a messenger angel in the night. And his harp strings rang true and honey sweet.

> *". . . This maiden outlaw bold and good*
> *With a wolf who gives her fealty,*
> *Daughter of fitting fatherhood:*
> *Rowan Hood of the rowan wood."*

In the firelit clearing around the great oak tree, outlaws stood or sat motionless, their flagons forgotten in their hands, their faces rapt and turned toward Lionel. Their mouths sagged open, softly agape. But Lionel saw no such softening in his father's face.

Go down there. Let him see you. Face him.

But he could not. Not yet. The thought set him to trembling again. He had to close his eyes against the sight of his father's stony face in order to sing on.

Singing to the dark, he finished the ballad of Rowan Hood and started another, the old, old song that had been his mother's favorite:

> *"Alas, my love, you do me wrong*
> *To cast me off discourteously . . ."*

9

A lion's roar of rage shattered his song, shook him worse than an earthquake, shook the branches above him. His hands faltered to a halt on his harp, and his throat tightened so badly that he could not sing, only squeak like a mouse. He knew that wordless bellow, although he had hoped never to hear it again.

"How dare you, sirrah!" Words, now, distorted by his father's fury.

With the shards of his song dying around him, Lionel looked. At his father. Lord Roderick Lionclaw, his face blood red in the firelight and creased in an agony of wrath. Lord Roderick Lionclaw, on his feet and lunging toward the darkness. "Churl!" Lionel's father roared, choking with rage. "Shameless! No son of mine! I will kill you!"

Half a dozen of Robin's men leapt to grasp Lord Roderick by the arms. Ablaze with fury, he threw two of them off and surged forward as if the other four were no more than fleas clinging to his hide. Outlaws cried out and seized their quarterstaffs. Linnets and thrushes cried out and flew up from their nests. It seemed to Lionel that the very oaks trembled. He shook so hard, he had to clutch his harp to keep from dropping it.

Three outlaws with quarterstaffs at the ready stood before Lord Roderick, warning him back, but he glared past them at the night, seeming not to see the cudgels. "Disgrace to my name!" he bellowed. "Show yourself!"

Face him, stand up to him! Be a man for once.

"Dare to show yourself, sirrah!" Throwing off the outlaws who held his massive warrior arm, Lionel's father shook his fist as if swinging his clawed mace. "I—will—*kill—you!*"

Lionel heard no more. Without knowing how his feet carried him, how he stood to run, or where he was going, he fled.

His throat had closed. He felt as if he would never be able to sing again.

Nancy Springer has loved fantasy since she read *King Arthur and His Knights*, edited by Philip Schuyler Allen, in her childhood. She has written over thirty-five novels for adults and children, and has won numerous awards, including two Edgar Allan Poe Awards. Her book *I Am Mordred* was named an American Library Association Best Book for Young Adults and won the 1999 Carolyn W. Field Award.